Buyer Beware . . .

"I've got three days to come up with a talent," Peter said. "And it has to be good."

"Don't worry," Crazy Merlin replied. "I've got just the thing for you. The Magician's Starter Kit."

That didn't sound like "just the thing" at all. In fact, it sounded pretty lame.

"What's in the Magician's Started Kit?" Peter asked. "Stupid handkerchief tricks
or something?"

"How dare you think I would sell 'stupid handkerchief tricks' at the Little Magic Shop of Horrors!" Crazy Merlin shot back. "That stuff is for sissies. Crazy Merlin the Mad Magician sells only tricks that are guaranteed to scare you to death!"

With that, there was a loud explosion and Crazy Merlin disappeared in a cloud of smoke.

LiTTLe MAGiC
SHOP OF HORRORS

ANNETTE CASCONE and GiNA CASCONE

A Tom Doherty Associates Book · New York

LITTLE MAGIC SHOP OF HORRORS

Copyright © 2012 by Annette Cascone and Gina Cascone

Grandpa's Monster Movies excerpt copyright © 2012 by Annette Cascone and Gina Cascone

Deadtime Stories® is a registered trademark of Annette Cascone and Gina Cascone.

Deadtime Stories logo by Bill Villareal

A Starscape Book
Published by Tom Doherty Associates, LLC
175 Fifth Avenue
New York, NY 10010

www.tor-forge.com

ISBN 978-0-7653-7095-2

Printed in the United States of America

S 0 9 8 7 6 5 4 3 2 1

To Richard Fazzari,

For always pointing out the sleight of hand—

no matter what the cost

DEADTIME STORIES

LITTLE MAGIC
SHOP OF HORRORS

1

Peter Newman twisted in his seat, squirming in unbearable pain. He held his hands tightly over his ears. Still, he couldn't escape the bloodcurdling sound.

Peter's best friend, Bo Wilson, tugged on his arm. "What does that sound like to you?" he asked over the hideous wailing.

Peter shrugged helplessly. He couldn't begin to describe the horrible noise.

Bo answered his own question. "It sounds like cats being slaughtered."

That was exactly what it sounded like! Murder. Pure, bloody murder.

Why isn't anybody putting a stop to this? Peter thought. *It's cruel and inhuman to allow this to continue.*

But continue it did.

More than two dozen people, Peter and Bo included, just sat there as Gerald MacDougal worked his instrument of torture.

"Bagpipes." Peter groaned. That was Gerald's evil instrument. "What kind of dweeb plays the bagpipes?" he went on, slumping down in his seat at the back of the school auditorium.

Bo laughed. "He's the worst act yet," he said in Peter's ear.

Peter had to agree. In the half hour since the school day had ended, he and Bo had seen some pretty awful acts, but Gerald MacDougal's was definitely the worst.

"The kid's got guts," Peter told Bo. "No talent, but a whole lot of guts."

"Too bad for him this is supposed to be a talent competition." Bo laughed even harder.

It was the audition for the school talent show. The show was being held at the end of the week, and twelve acts would be chosen. But judging from what he'd seen so far, Peter didn't think it was going to be much of a competition.

Bo was enjoying it, though. He was having a great time making fun of all the kids up on stage. He'd even brought along snacks.

As Gerald gave one last agonizing yowl on the bagpipes, Bo tore into the wrapper of another candy bar. He broke it in two, handing half to Peter. Then he tossed the empty wrapper over his shoulder.

"Don't throw the garbage on the floor," Peter scolded him. "We'll get into trouble. We're not even supposed to be eating in here."

"Nobody's paying attention to us," Bo said as the teachers sitting in the front row politely applauded Gerald's awful performance. "Who cares about—"

"What's this?" A deep voice cut off Bo's words.

Bo was wrong. Somebody *was* paying attention to them.

Peter and Bo froze in their seats, eyes straight ahead. Neither of them had the courage to turn around and face the voice.

The discarded candy wrapper dropped from above into Bo's lap. Still, neither Peter nor Bo moved.

"No eating in the auditorium," the voice said.

Peter glanced over his shoulder. The school janitor loomed over them.

Janitor Bob was more than six feet tall and was built like a professional football player. But for someone so big, he moved as silently as a shadow. He was always appearing out of nowhere to catch kids doing what they shouldn't be doing. This time he'd caught the two of them.

"That's strike two," Janitor Bob said, holding up two enormous gloved fingers.

"Strike two?" Bo repeated, practically jumping out of his seat. "How can that be strike two?" he protested. "We don't even have a strike one."

"Oh really?" Janitor Bob glared down at them. "Who drew the lovely picture of Mrs. Dingleman on the mirror in the boys' room last week?"

Mrs. Dingleman was the principal. And the picture in the boys' room wasn't "lovely" at all. It was actually pretty rude.

Peter and Bo exchanged guilty looks. But neither said a word.

"One more strike and you're out," Janitor Bob whispered menacingly. Then he turned around and headed through the back doors of the auditorium as silently as he'd entered.

"Oh man." Bo sighed. "No way Psycho Bob knows we drew that picture."

"Yes, way!" Peter shot back. "Didn't you hear what he said?"

Every kid in school was scared of Janitor Bob. Because every kid in the school knew that he had superhuman strength and a superexplosive temper. Peter had heard that Janitor Bob once lifted an entire school bus by himself, just to move it out of his parking spot. Even if the story wasn't true, Janitor Bob was not somebody Peter wanted to mess with.

"What do you suppose happens when you get three strikes?" Peter asked nervously.

"I don't know," Bo answered. "Nobody's ever gotten three strikes before. At least nobody who's lived to tell about it. For all I know, he may just kill you and bury you in that basement office of his."

"Don't drop any more wrappers," Peter ordered Bo. "There's no way I want to get three strikes."

"Okay, okay," Bo said. "Now shut up. We're missing the whole show."

The next act was almost over. It was two girls from Peter's class dancing around the stage in frilly tutus. They looked pretty silly. But they'd finished their dance before Peter and Bo could start making fun of them.

"Look who's up next." Bo nudged Peter with his elbow.

"Oh, puke!" Peter groaned. "It's Mary-Margaret Mahoney." He spit out the name like he was spitting out poison. "I hate that girl."

"Me too," Bo said. "She thinks she's such hot stuff."

The two of them cringed as Mary-Margaret Mahoney strutted onto the stage in a bright red, rhinestone-studded cowgirl costume, carrying a baton.

"Oh, brother," Peter said. "She's going to twirl her stupid baton again."

"Of course she is," Bo told him. "It's the only talent she's got."

Peter laughed. "So what's she going to be when she grows up—a professional baton twirler?"

"No," Bo answered. "She's going to be Miss America. Remember? That's what she always tells everybody."

"Not with that face, she isn't," Peter said. "I'd be surprised if she could win a dog show."

"For real," Bo agreed. "But she's been bragging all week about how she's going to win the school talent show. She just might do it, too. It's not like she has any competition. Besides, she really does know how to twirl that baton. She's even won state competitions."

"I know, I know." Peter rolled his eyes. "Every time she gets her stupid picture in the paper, Mrs. Dingleman puts it up on the bulletin board. Then Mary-Margaret walks around like she really *is* Miss America. If she wins this show, she'll be totally obnoxious about it."

"Well, she's going to win," Bo said. "Look." He pointed toward the stage.

Mary-Margaret was standing at the foot of the stage.

She handed her baton to her mother, who'd been whispering something to the teachers who were judging. Peter watched as Mrs. Dingleman, the head judge, nodded at Mrs. Mahoney.

A second later, Mrs. Mahoney lit the baton on fire and handed it back to Mary-Margaret.

"A fire baton!" Peter was shocked. "I can't believe they're letting her do a fire baton in school."

"They let Mary-Margaret do anything she wants to do," Bo griped. "Besides, it's the fire baton that always wins her the state competitions. The judges think it's great."

"If Mary-Margaret gets to dance around with fire, she's sure to win." Peter moaned.

Bo grinned. "Not if we do something to mess her up."

"Like what?" Peter asked.

Bo didn't answer. He was too busy fishing around inside his backpack. A second later, he pulled out a rubber band and a bag of peanut M&M's.

Mary-Margaret's hoedown music started to play. Within seconds, her silver baton was a fiery blur. She passed it behind her back and under her leg. Then she tossed it high up into the air and caught it.

With every trick, the judges burst into loud applause. Mary-Margaret danced around the stage, smiling smugly.

But not for long.

Bo loaded a peanut M&M into the slingshot he'd created with the rubber band and his fingers. He took careful aim and let it rip.

A second later, catastrophe struck. But as Peter watched, it felt as if it were happening in slow motion.

Mary-Margaret had turned sideways. She'd lifted her leg to pass her fire baton beneath it. Suddenly the peanut M&M hit her in the butt, and Mary-Margaret let out a loud squeal. The fire baton flew into the air, twirling out of control.

Peter started to laugh. He thought it was the funniest thing he'd ever seen—until the swirling ball of flames slammed right into the stage curtains.

2

Mrs. Dingleman and the other teachers jumped out of their seats, screaming in terror as a giant flame licked its way up the curtain.

The rhinestone-studded beauty queen cowgirl dove off the stage into her mother's arms, crying hysterically.

Peter and Bo sat glued to their seats, watching in stunned disbelief.

"Call nine-one-one!" Mrs. Dingleman cried.

"Just pull the fire alarm," another teacher yelled, running for the alarm box near the door.

"Let me out of here!" Gerald MacDougal screamed. He leapt out of his seat and ran down the aisle, dragging his bagpipes behind him.

The panic was contagious. Within seconds, the auditorium was full of commotion.

"Everybody calm down." A deep, booming voice rose above the hysterics as Janitor Bob stepped out from behind the flaming curtains. "There's no problem," he assured everyone. "Just give me a minute and I'll have this whole situation under control."

"Where the heck did he come from?" Peter gasped.

"From behind the curtains," Bo answered dumbly.

"I know that," Peter muttered. "I meant, how did he get there so fast? He just went through the back doors a few seconds ago."

Peter looked at the door behind them, then down at the stage where Janitor Bob stood. It was impossible for him to have gotten onstage that quickly.

"Who knows?" Bo shrugged. "Maybe he beamed in."

"He must have," Peter said. Then he watched Janitor Bob do something even more impossible. He stepped right into the flames shooting out from the curtain, took one deep breath, and blew out the fire.

"Geez, oh, man!" Peter blinked hard. "Did you see that?"

"He just blew the whole thing out!" Bo exclaimed in amazement.

The curtains weren't even singed.

Janitor Bob bent down and picked up the fire baton from the stage floor. Then he blew that out, too.

"Oh, Bob!" Mrs. Dingleman exclaimed. "You're an absolute miracle worker!"

"Not really." Janitor Bob smiled. "These curtains are fire resistant. The flame was skittering along the surface of the material. I'm just glad I got to them before the fire really caught."

"Amazing." Mrs. Dingleman sighed. "You're absolutely amazing. I don't know what we would do around here without you."

"Nice of you to say so." Janitor Bob nodded politely to Mrs. Dingleman. But his dark, piercing eyes were focused on the back row of the auditorium.

Peter bent his head down, trying to escape Janitor Bob's glare. But his eyes were like magnets. Peter couldn't break the gaze.

Janitor Bob held up three fingers.

Strike three! Peter's stomach lurched. *Janitor Bob wasn't even in the auditorium when Bo shot the M&M at Mary-Margaret,* he thought. *How could he possibly know what we did?*

"Let's get out of here!" Bo was panicking big time. "Before Psycho Bob comes after us."

"Good idea," Peter quickly agreed.

The two of them were out of their seats and through the back doors of the auditorium like a shot.

"This way." Peter tugged on Bo's sleeve, pulling him to the back exit of the school building. Unfortunately, the doors were locked. They doubled back toward the front of the school. The coast was clear. It looked like luck was on their side. . . .

Until they burst through the front doors.

"Fire trucks!" Bo gasped. "Somebody must have pulled the alarm!"

But the fire trucks were the least of their worries. Standing on the walkway blocking their escape was Janitor Bob, looking more like a madman than a miracle worker.

3

"T hat's it!" Janitor Bob grabbed Peter and Bo by their collars. "I'm done playing games with the two of you!"

"What games?" Bo blurted out in a panic. "We're not playing any games, Janitor Bob—honest!"

"It's time to take a little walk down to my office," Janitor Bob snarled.

With that news, Peter's pounding heart came to a stop. But his brain started pumping like crazy. *Three strikes and you're worse than out. You're dead!*

"I don't want to go down to the basement!" Peter cried aloud.

"Too bad," Janitor Bob said. "Because that's where you're going." He began marching them forward.

"Why don't you just take us to the principal's office instead?" Peter pleaded. The thought of getting suspended was a whole lot better than the thought of getting dead.

"Yeah," Bo agreed. "Why don't you just take us to Mrs. Dingleman? I promise I'll confess. I'll even tell her about the picture in the boys' room if you want."

"Sorry, pal." Janitor Bob shook his head. "You aren't getting off that easy. Besides, I like to take care of my problems all by myself."

Peter gulped.

"But don't worry about keeping this from Mrs. Dingleman," Janitor Bob went on, dragging them back toward the building. "Because I promise you, justice will be served."

Justice? What kind of justice? Psycho janitor justice?

Peter could see the blood draining from Bo's face as they exchanged terrified glances.

"Now you two M&M-shooting pyros keep your lips shut and your eyes straight ahead when we enter this building. You got me?" It wasn't a question. It was a threat.

Peter and Bo nodded. They walked along quietly as Janitor Bob steered them down the deserted hallway to the giant locked door that led to the basement.

As Janitor Bob reached for his keys, Peter shot Bo a look Bo understood. It was time to beat it out of there.

But before they'd taken even one step, Janitor Bob's massive fingers wrapped around their collars again. "Now that's three and a half," he barked. "And even I don't know what kind of punishment you should get for three and a half strikes."

Three and a half! This guy was out of his mind! What was he going to do? Kill them one and a half times?

"Move it," he ordered, shoving Peter and Bo through the open doorway in front of him.

Peter stared down at the cracked, crumbling steps that led to the basement. There wasn't even a railing. And the stairwell was so dimly lit, it really did look like the entrance to some janitorial torture chamber. It didn't help Peter's nerves when Janitor Bob shut and locked the door behind them.

"Take a left at the bottom," Janitor Bob instructed as they reached the landing.

It figures, Peter thought. The right side of the base-ment was brightly lit with dozens of fluorescent bulbs, but the left side was dark, dingy, and dank. One lone light bulb flickered above them.

"Oh man," Bo whispered as they inched their way toward an old door with a glow-in-the-dark sign that read JANITOR BOB'S OFFICE. "We're dead!"

"Not yet you're not," Janitor Bob snapped back. "But you will be if you keep up that yapping."

Bo let out a tiny yip before all yapping stopped.

When Janitor Bob pushed open the door to his of-fice, the first thing Peter saw was a collection of yearbook pictures taped to the cinder-block walls. Big red Xs were drawn through some of the faces—faces Peter didn't rec-ognize.

That's because they're probably all dead and buried un-derneath my feet! Peter thought. He almost hit the ceiling as Janitor Bob closed and locked the office door behind him.

"Now you two clowns put your behinds in those chairs and don't even breathe." Janitor Bob pointed to the wooden seats in front of his metal desk.

Peter and Bo did as they were told.

"Where the heck *is* that thing?" Janitor Bob mumbled to himself as he dug through the mountains of papers and tools he had on his desk.

What thing? Peter shot Bo a worried look.

"Dang it," Janitor Bob huffed, tossing what looked like a bone-crunching, viselike tool to the floor. "I must have left it in the washroom."

Janitor Bob reached for the door by the side of his desk. It looked like a closet. But when he pulled open the door, Peter could see that it wasn't a closet at all. It was a long dark hallway.

"Stay put," Janitor Bob ordered, stepping through the door. "I'll be right back."

As Janitor Bob disappeared into the darkness, Bo whispered frantically, "He's probably looking for his ax so he can chop us up into little pieces."

Peter wanted to scream for help, but he knew no one would hear them. No one but Janitor Bob.

"We have to get out of here!" Bo cried.

Just then, Peter heard footsteps outside. Someone was coming. Someone who might be able to save them!

But as Peter opened his mouth to scream, another set of footsteps made him stay silent.

"Got it," Janitor Bob announced, appearing from the hallway. *It* was a big red book about the size of an encyclopedia. It zippered all the way around, so there was no way to tell what was inside it.

"Hello?" a voice behind the office door called out. "I'm looking for Janitor Bob."

Bo heaved a sigh of relief.

So did Peter. *Maybe it's the police*, he hoped.

Janitor Bob slowly headed for the door. He unlocked it, then pulled it open just a crack.

Peter craned his neck to see who it was.

Unfortunately, it wasn't the police. It was Bernie, from Bernie's Bicycle Shop. Peter recognized him right away. He was standing outside in the hallway with two brand-new, incredible-looking ten-speed mountain bikes by his side.

What the heck is Bernie doing here? Peter wondered.

"Are you Janitor Bob?" Bernie asked.

Janitor Bob nodded.

"I've got the prizes for the winner of the school's talent

contest," Bernie said. "Mrs. Dingleman said you should store them down here until Friday."

"Sure thing," Janitor Bob told him. "You can just leave them right there. I'll lock them up when I'm through here."

No way! Peter thought. *Mary-Margaret Mahoney's going to get a ten-speed mountain bike for twirling a baton?* The two bikes that Bernie had brought weren't just any mountain bikes, either. They were exactly the kind of bike Peter had been wanting for months.

He was so irritated by the thought of Mary-Margaret Mahoney winning the talent contest and getting one of those bikes, he almost forgot how scared he was. Until Janitor Bob closed the door.

"Okay, you two." Janitor Bob turned his attention back to the boys. He unzipped his book and began skimming through the pages. "Here's what you're in for."

Oh man, Peter thought. *He's looking up some new and improved torture for us in his janitorial torture book.*

Bo gulped so loudly, it echoed off the walls.

Finally, Janitor Bob found the punishment that fit the crime.

"What is it?" Bo asked out loud.

"Window cleaning," Janitor Bob announced, glaring at them.

"*Window cleaning?*" Peter repeated. *That was it? That was their torture? Impossible*, Peter thought. *There has to be a catch.*

There was.

"That's right," Janitor Bob said. "Window cleaning—on Saturday. But if you don't think that's punishment enough, I'm sure I'll be able to come up with something much more creative." He laughed wickedly. "And it's going to be just the three of us here. So your moaning and groaning won't bother a soul."

4

W hat are we going to do?" Bo was already moaning and groaning as they headed for Peter's house. "I don't want to go to school on Saturday to get killed by Janitor Bob!"

"Janitor Bob's not going to kill us," Peter assured Bo, even though he wasn't so sure himself.

"Right," Bo said. "Maybe he'll just torture us."

"He's not going to torture us, either," Peter said. "He's not going to do anything to us. Because we're not going to school on Saturday."

"What are you, nuts?" Bo cried. "If we don't go,

Psycho Bob's going to hunt us down and make us 'sorry we were ever born,'" he said, repeating Janitor Bob's threat.

"Then we have to go to Mrs. Dingleman and tell her what you did," Peter decided.

"What I did?" Bo snapped. "It's not like I was sitting there by myself!" he reminded Peter.

"I'm not the one who shot Mary-Margaret with an M&M," Peter said.

"No. But you wanted me to do it," Bo said. "And I'll tell Mrs. Dingleman that, too."

"Look," Peter huffed. "We're in this thing together, okay? So let's just figure a way out of it."

"Fine," Bo said. "But we can't tell Mrs. Dingleman."

"Why not?" Peter asked.

"Because Mrs. Dingleman will call my parents. And *they'll* kill me even *worse* than Janitor Bob. You've got it easy," he told Peter. "If Mrs. Dingleman calls your house, she'll get Grandma Grussler."'

Peter's parents were away for a week on a business trip. Grandma Grussler, Peter's mom's mom, was staying with Peter until they got back.

Peter couldn't believe his parents had left Grandma Grussler in charge. Not because he *didn't* like her, but because he *did*. In fact, he got a big kick out of her. Grandma Grussler was "eccentric"—at least that's what everyone said she was. And while Peter wasn't quite sure what that meant, he had the feeling it was just another way of saying that Grandma Grussler was totally off of her rocker.

Bo was right. He did have it easy. If Mrs. Dingleman called Grandma Grussler, she'd forget all about it two seconds later.

"I'm telling you," Bo kept moaning. "If my parents find out I set the auditorium on fire, I might as well just bury *myself* in Janitor Bob's office."

"You didn't set the auditorium on fire," Peter pointed out. "You shot Mary-Margaret with an M&M."

"Same thing," Bo insisted.

Just the thought of Mary-Margaret winning first prize sent Peter into a tailspin. "I can't believe she's going to get one of those bikes on Friday," he griped. "I'm not going to sit there and watch that butt-kissing, backstabbing little creep get my bike."

Bo looked anxiously at Peter. "Oh, no," he said. "Don't even think about it. Because I'm not doing it!"

"Doing what?" Peter asked.

"Whatever it is you're thinking about doing," he told Peter.

Peter shared his bright idea anyway. "We're going to enter that talent contest and win," he told Bo.

Bo cracked up. "What are you going to do? Borrow Gerald MacDougal's bagpipes?"

"I'm serious," Peter said. "There's got to be something we can do to beat Mary-Margaret and her baton."

"We?" Bo raised his eyebrow. "What do you mean 'we'?"

"Me and you," Peter said. "We can do something together."

"I don't think so." Bo laughed. "Gerald MacDougal's got more talent than you. And the only thing I know how to do is burp the National Anthem. Trust me," he went on. "The judges won't like it. Besides, there's no way I'm getting up on that stage to make a fool of myself."

"You are if you want me to take half the rap for

setting the auditorium on fire," Peter threatened. "If you don't enter the talent show with me so we can win those bikes, I'll tell Mrs. Dingleman everything."

"You wouldn't dare," Bo gasped.

"Would too," Peter lied.

"Fine," Bo snapped as they headed up Peter's driveway. "We'll enter the stupid talent contest. But you'd better learn how to burp real good."

"We're not going to burp," Peter told him. "We're going to do something else. Something great."

"Like what?" Bo demanded.

"I don't know," Peter said, opening his front door. "But I'll figure it out before Friday."

"You don't have until Friday," Bo pointed out. "The last day for auditions is Thursday. So you'd better figure it out by then."

As Peter and Bo stepped into the family room, Grandma Grussler called from the kitchen.

"Paulie?" she said. "Is that you, dear?"

"No, Grandma," Peter called back. "It's me, Peter."

"Who's Paulie?" Bo asked.

"One of my uncles," Peter said. "She's always calling

me that. Or Joey. Or Sonny. She has seven kids and twelve grandchildren. She's always getting our names mixed up."

"How old's your uncle Paulie?" Bo asked.

"Forty-two," Peter answered.

"And she can't tell you apart?"

Peter just shrugged as he headed for the kitchen.

Grandma Grussler was standing by the kitchen counter reaching into a box of doggy biscuits. One side of her shiny blue hair was rolled up in curlers, the other was sticking straight up. Her knee-high stockings were where they always were, rolled down to her ankles. And her polka-dotted apron was tied around her waist backward.

"I've got yum-yums for you, Tiger," Grandma Grussler said, waving a doggy biscuit in front of Tiger's nose.

Tiger was Grandma Grussler's "traveling companion." He was also a cat.

Bo glanced at Peter out of the corner of his eye. "Why's she giving the cat *doggy* biscuits?" he whispered.

Peter didn't bother to answer Bo's question. He didn't know why Grandma Grussler fed doggy biscuits to her cat. "Hi, Grandma," he said as he stepped into the kitchen. "You remember Bo, don't you?"

"Oh, sure I remember." Grandma Grussler smiled at Bo. "You're Sonny's little friend."

"No, I'm . . ."

Peter nudged Bo hard. It was easier to let Grandma Grussler believe what she wanted to believe. Otherwise they'd be stuck in the kitchen for hours while she tried to pull her head back together. "Yeah, Grandma," Peter said. "Bo is Sonny's little friend."

The orange-and-black-striped cat took one sniff of the doggy biscuit and bolted out of the kitchen.

"So how was school for my favorite grandson today?" Grandma Grussler asked.

"Good," Peter lied.

"Anything exciting happen?"

"Nope," Peter answered.

"Just a fire in the auditorium," Bo mumbled under his breath.

Peter was about to start laughing—until Grandma Grussler gasped. "A fire?" she said, clutching her heart.

"It was nothing, Grandma," Peter assured her, giving

Bo a dirty look. "Some girl was twirling a fire baton and a spark landed on the curtains. The janitor blew it out right away."

"Yeah," Bo jumped in. "It was no big deal."

"Thank heavens." Grandma Grussler sighed. "You had me worried for a second. Fires are not fun to be around. Believe you me."

Just then, Peter noticed smoke billowing out from the oven door. "Uh, Grandma . . ." He pointed to the oven. "Speaking of fires, I think something's burning in there."

"Oh, dear!" Grandma Grussler reached for her mitts. "My fruitcake."

"Speaking of fruitcakes," Bo muttered in Peter's ear as Grandma Grussler pulled open the oven door.

"Look at this," she cried, pulling out the pan. "It's burned to a crisp."

Hooray! Peter thought. *Now I won't have to eat it.*

"I followed every word of those darn directions," Grandma Grussler went on. " 'Easy,' my butt!" she griped. "You have to be a magician to bake one of these things."

Magician!

The moment Peter heard the word, he knew exactly what he and Bo could do in the talent show. "A magic act!" he blurted out.

"Exactly," Grandma Grussler said. "Making an elephant disappear would be easier than baking this fruitcake."

"No, Grandma," Peter said. "That's not what I meant. Bo and I are going to win a couple of bikes!"

Bo shot Peter a look.

"That's good, dear," she said, paying more attention to her smoking cake than to Peter.

"Come on," he told Bo. "I know just where to look to find what we need." He grabbed Bo by the shirt and pulled him out of the kitchen. "We'll be upstairs if you need us, Grandma," he called over his shoulder.

A few minutes later, Peter found exactly what he was looking for in the yellow pages of the phone book.

"Check it out," he told Bo, pointing to a full–page ad with dripping red letters. "We're bound to find something in this place that'll get us into the talent show. I can't wait to kick Mary-Margaret's fire-baton-twirling butt!"

Bo smiled as he stared at the page.

No doubt about it. They were definitely going to find something more awesome than a fire baton at the Little Magic Shop of Horrors.

5

There is no magic shop," Bo said, plunking himself down on the curb in front of the pharmacy on Main Street.

"It's got to be here somewhere," Peter replied. "The ad in the phone book said it was right off Main Street."

"We've been up and down this street a dozen times," Bo complained. "I told you it was a joke. There is no such place as 101 Nosuch Place!"

"There's got to be," Peter insisted. He'd even called the magic shop to make sure the address was right. "The guy on the phone said it's right in the middle of town. He also said it's been here forever."

"Then how come we've never seen it before?" Bo asked.

"Because we've never looked," Peter said impatiently. Then he pulled Bo to his feet and dragged him back down the street again. "It's got to be here somewhere," he persisted, crossing the first side street.

"Well, this is Green Street," Bo said, reading the sign. "And we've already crossed it about six thousand times."

The next street was Magnolia. After that came Elm.

"It's useless," Bo declared.

Peter was about to agree when something up ahead caught his eye. There was an archway in the solid brick wall of shop fronts. It was right between the bookstore and the ladies' shoe shop. Peter had never noticed it before.

"Look," he told Bo, heading toward it.

"What is that?" Bo asked. "An alleyway?"

There was a sign above the arch. Peter smiled as he

read what it said. "It's Nosuch Place!" he exclaimed, pointing the plaque out to Bo.

"Too weird," Bo said. "I didn't see this archway before."

"Me neither," Peter agreed, stepping through it. "I'm just glad we finally found it."

Nosuch Place wasn't really a street. It wasn't an alleyway, either. It was more like a tunnel.

When Peter and Bo came out the other end, they found themselves in a tiny courtyard. It was so small, Peter felt as if he were standing inside an air shaft. Solid brick walls surrounded them on all four sides.

"What a creepy place to put a store," Peter said, looking around.

Bo nodded in agreement. "And look at the store."

The shop looming in front of them looked as if it had been closed for a hundred years. The front window was covered with so much grime, Peter couldn't see inside.

But it was definitely the right place. It said so on the window, in bright red letters that looked as if they'd been written in dripping blood.

"Do you really want to go in there?" Bo sounded unsure.

"Are you kidding?" Peter said. "This is going to be great."

When he pulled open the door and stepped through it, a tinny-sounding bell jingled overhead. He looked up at it as Bo followed him inside.

The store appeared to be deserted. In fact, it looked as though no one had been inside the place in years. Everything was buried under inches of dust, including the floor. Peter and Bo left footprints as they walked.

"Hello," Peter called out nervously. "Is anybody here?"

There was no answer.

"Maybe we should leave," Bo suggested.

"No way," Peter told him. "Not until we take a look around. There's a lot of cool stuff in here. Check this out." Peter pointed to a life-size skeleton standing behind the door.

"Gross!" Bo cried. "He's got eyeballs."

"That's what makes him so cool." Peter laughed. He walked closer to the skeleton to get a better look.

As Peter moved, so did the skeleton's eyeballs. They seemed to be following him. "Neat trick," Peter said. "I wonder how it works."

"There are probably batteries in there that make the eyes move around," Bo said.

Peter supposed that was right. Still, it was pretty eerie the way the eyes seemed to follow his every move. Peter stared up at the skeleton for a couple of seconds before turning his attention to other things in the store.

"Look at this." He headed over to a black box that was almost as big as a phone booth.

"What's that?" Bo asked, coming up beside Peter.

"I'll bet it's a disappearing box," Peter told him, opening the door.

"How do you suppose it works?" Bo asked.

"I think there's a secret compartment behind one of the walls," Peter answered. "When the magician closes the door, the person in the box hides in the secret compartment. Then, when the magician opens the box again, the person inside seems to have disappeared."

"It doesn't look like there's any place to hide inside this box," Bo said as he examined the walls.

Peter felt around for himself. Bo was right. The walls were pretty solid. It didn't look as though there was a secret compartment.

But there had to be. It was the only way the trick could work.

"Maybe the door has to be closed before the secret compartment will open," Peter said. "Go inside and try," he told Bo.

"Are you nuts?" Bo shook his head. "I'm not letting you close me in that box. *You* do it."

Peter didn't like the idea of being shut inside a dark box, either. But it would be worth it if he could make himself disappear—just to scare Bo.

"Fine." He stepped into the box. "Close the door and count to twenty," he told Bo.

Confident that the secret compartment would be at the back of the box, Peter faced the back wall as Bo closed the door.

Peter was surprised at how dark it got. It was pitch-black. He closed his eyes tight to block out the darkness. Then he began feeling around for the secret compartment.

He could hear Bo counting outside the box. "Four . . . five . . . six . . ."

Peter pushed against the back wall, hard. "Come on," he said. But the wall wouldn't give.

Maybe it was one of the side walls. Peter slid his hand along the back wall until he got to a corner and then turned to face the side wall.

"Eleven . . . twelve . . . thirteen . . ." Bo kept right on counting.

It was useless. The side wall wasn't budging, either. But Peter wasn't about to give up yet. There was one last wall to try and not much time.

He turned around to face the other side wall. He took a step forward, reaching his hands out in front of him, his eyes still closed.

He was surprised when he didn't feel the wall—so surprised that he opened his eyes. It didn't help; it was still pitch-black.

He stretched his arms out farther as he took another step. No wall . . . but—

A scream exploded from Peter's throat.

Something was in the box with him—and it was alive!

6

What's wrong?" Bo shouted as he threw open the door to the disappearing box.

Peter flew out of the box as if he'd been fired from a cannon. For a second, he was blinded by the light. He couldn't see a thing. Behind him came the sound of terrible laughter—laughter that was soon drowned out by Bo's screams.

Peter blinked hard to focus his eyes. Finally, he saw what it was that was making Bo scream.

A big man had stepped out of the box. He was dressed in a suit and wearing dark glasses with lightning bolts shooting off the sides. He was also wearing a broad, toothy grin.

"Calm down," he told the boys. "I'm not going to hurt you." He took a step toward them. "I'm Crazy Merlin. Welcome to my Little Magic Shop of Horrors."

"You scared the daylights out of me," Peter scolded him.

Crazy Merlin started laughing again. "It's my favorite trick," he said. "Guaranteed to shake up the customers every time."

"How did you do that?" Bo asked suspiciously. He was looking past Crazy Merlin into the disappearing box.

"Magic," Crazy Merlin whispered.

"That was a pretty good trick," Peter was forced to admit. "It was as if you appeared out of nowhere."

"I did," Crazy Merlin said. "After all, I am a master magician."

He didn't look like a master magician. In fact, except for his wild sunglasses, Crazy Merlin looked like a pretty ordinary guy.

"How did you even know we were in here?" Bo asked.

"I always keep my eye on the door," Crazy Merlin told them.

"But you were hiding inside that box," Bo said.

"*I* was in the box," Crazy Merlin replied. "But my eyes were on the door."

Peter and Bo exchanged confused looks. This guy wasn't called *Crazy* Merlin for nothing.

"Let me show you how I do it," Crazy Merlin said.

The two boys watched as Merlin walked over to the skeleton they'd seen when they first came in. Then he reached up and popped the eyeballs right out of the skeleton's head.

"See?" he said, turning back to Peter and Bo. He had an eyeball in the palm of each hand, holding them out for the boys' inspection.

Peter watched as the eyeballs rolled around for a minute in Crazy Merlin's palms. If Crazy Merlin was moving them, Peter couldn't tell how. His hands seemed to be perfectly still.

Finally, the eyeballs stopped. They fixed on Peter with a terrible stare.

Peter shivered, then took a step back.

So did Bo. "Gross," he said. "Those things look real."

"That's because they *are* real," Crazy Merlin told him.

The eyeballs shifted toward Bo.

"Cool!" Peter said. It was an amazing trick. He wanted to know how Crazy Merlin did it.

"Let me see," Peter said, reaching for an eyeball.

Now it was Crazy Merlin who stepped away. "Sorry," he said. "I can't let you do that. It's time to put these baby blues back where they belong."

Crazy Merlin turned his back. He took off his glasses, then popped the eyeballs into his own head!

7

Peter watched dumbfounded as the eyeballs rolled around in Crazy Merlin's head.

"Knock it off," Bo pleaded, covering his own eyes. "This is too gross for words!"

"It's what we call an *optical* illusion." Crazy Merlin laughed at his joke, then his eyes focused on Peter. "Don't you like my little eyeball trick?"

Peter nodded. "How do you do it?" he asked cautiously.

"Like this," Crazy Merlin answered, putting his hand to his face. In less than a second, he had one eye closed and an eyeball in the palm of his hand. "Here," he said, holding it out to Peter. "Take it."

"Do it," Bo urged, peeking at Peter through his fingers. "See if it's real."

"Of course it's not real," Peter told Bo. "People can't pop *real* eyeballs in and out of their heads. Can they?" He looked nervously at Crazy Merlin.

"You never know." Merlin grinned.

Peter was almost too afraid to touch the eyeball in Merlin's hand. But he had to prove to himself that it really was just a trick. He held out his hand. As Crazy Merlin dropped the eyeball into his palm, it landed with a *splat*.

Peter was so repelled, he almost hurled it across the room. Then he realized something. "It's not an eyeball. It's a marble." He heaved a sigh of relief.

Bo leaned in to look for himself. As he did, Peter jiggled his hand, and the eyeball moved. Bo let out a scream. Peter cracked up.

"You're such a jerk," Bo grumbled.

Peter did feel like a jerk. Not for scaring Bo, but for thinking that the eyeball was real in the first place. So far the Little Magic Shop of Horrors was definitely living up to its name.

"You got us pretty good with that trick," Peter said to Crazy Merlin. He held out the eyeball to give it back.

"Keep it," Merlin told him. "I've got plenty more." He went behind the counter and pulled out a huge glass jar filled with eyeballs of every color. He fished around inside it and pulled out a purple one. "My favorite color." He smiled at the boys. Then he popped it right into his head.

Peter couldn't believe his eyes. Crazy Merlin was now staring at them with one blue eye and one purple eye.

"You have to teach me how to do this!" Peter told Crazy Merlin. "There's a talent competition at school, and first prize is a mountain bike. If I could do the eyeball trick, we'd win for sure."

"I couldn't possibly teach you this trick," Crazy Merlin answered. "Only master magicians can perform the seeing-eyeball trick. It takes years of practice."

"I don't have years." Peter sighed. "I've got three days to come up with a talent. And it has to be good."

"Don't worry," Crazy Merlin replied. "I've got just the thing for you. The Magician's Starter Kit."

That didn't sound like "just the thing" at all. In fact, it sounded pretty lame. "What's in the Magician's Starter Kit?" Peter asked. "Stupid handkerchief tricks or something?"

"How dare you think I would sell 'stupid handkerchief tricks' at the Little Magic Shop of Horrors!" Crazy Merlin shot back. "That stuff is for sissies. Crazy Merlin the Mad Magician sells only tricks that are guaranteed to scare you to death!"

With that, there was a loud explosion and Crazy Merlin disappeared in a cloud of smoke.

8

"Where'd he go?" Bo asked, looking around the shop.

A door squeaked on its hinges. Peter spun toward the sound.

"I'm right here," Crazy Merlin said, stepping through the doorway along the far wall. "I had to pop into my office to get a couple of things."

"This guy's good," Peter whispered to Bo.

Crazy Merlin headed over to where they stood with several items in his hands. "These are the most important tools of the trade," he told them as he placed the items on top of the counter. "First, the magician's wand."

It looked like an ordinary old wand, a black stick

with a white tip. But there was a clear stone set into the very end of it that looked like a cut-glass prism.

Pretty neat, Peter thought, picking up the wand.

"The wand directs the magician's power," Crazy Merlin explained. "But beware. Unless the magician has complete control, the wand may bring surprising results."

"Abracadabra," Peter said, waving the stick at Bo. "Change my friend into a toad."

"Hey!" Bo jumped back.

Peter cracked up.

"Watch yourself," Crazy Merlin scolded. "Magic is no laughing matter."

"Sorry," Peter mumbled. He put down the wand and tried to look serious.

"Next, the magician's ring." Crazy Merlin pointed to it. "The ring gives power to whoever wears it."

Peter picked it up and put it on his finger. It was too big for his ring finger. He stuck it on his first finger, where it fit just right.

"Nice," Peter said. But he didn't really mean it. The

ring was kind of cheesy-looking—fake silver with a big, fake, multicolored stone.

"And last but not least," Merlin went on, "we have the magician's amulet." He lifted a goofy-looking necklace off the counter. "The amulet protects the magician so that his commands are followed exactly."

"This is the Starter Kit?" Peter asked, feeling more than a little disappointed. "I'm going to need a lot more than this to win the talent competition."

"And you're going to get a lot more," Crazy Merlin assured him. "Just remember, without these three things, you're nothing but a joke."

"What I really need are some scary tricks," Peter said.

"Scary's no good," Crazy Merlin told him, shaking his head.

"Why not?" Bo asked.

"Because horrifying is better!" Merlin's eyeballs rolled around in their sockets again as he laughed wildly. "Now close your eyes and count to ten while I gather up some terrifying tools of the trade."

Peter glanced at Bo.

"Close them!" Crazy Merlin ordered.

Peter and Bo did as they were told.

As they started to count, Peter heard all kinds of bangs and clangs coming from the corners of the room. But he didn't dare disobey Merlin's orders—until he felt something whiz by his head. It was so close, Peter could feel his hair moving as it blew past his scalp. He opened one eye and looked up.

Above him, six shiny daggers flew through the air as if they'd been thrown from behind him. But Crazy Merlin was standing in front of him. The pointed blades were headed straight for Merlin's face.

"Look out!" Peter screamed. He ducked fast, pulling Bo down with him.

Crazy Merlin laughed as he caught the blade of a dagger between his teeth. In front of him stood a towering pile of swords and head-chopping blades. "You're peeking," he said.

"How'd you do that?" Bo gasped.

"That's for me to know, and you to find out," the magician said. "Hopefully not the hard way."

"The daggers fly by themselves?" Peter asked.

"Only if you command them to," Crazy Merlin answered. "But I wouldn't try catching them with your teeth unless you're sure you've got total control. Besides," he added, "the daggers are really for the Wheel of Torture. Don't worry, I'll give you that, too."

Peter and Bo exchanged looks as Crazy Merlin headed back around the counter.

"Now, here are some bone-crunching handcuffs, fake peeling flesh, and oozing red blood capsules." He piled them onto the counter. "You'll also need the disappearing box, of course. It doubles as the Box of Death. Just stick those swords right through your friend," he said, pointing to the pile on the floor. "The head-chopping blades are self-explanatory. Here, take a couple of eyeballs, too—just don't put them in your eye sockets yet." He took a handful out of the jar and put them with the rest of the stuff. "I'll even throw in a stupid handkerchief trick. Now *that's* the Magician's Starter Kit."

"How much does all this stuff cost?" Peter asked.

"Nine ninety-five," Merlin told him.

"Nine hundred and ninety-five dollars?" Bo gasped.

"No," Merlin answered. "Nine dollars and ninety-five cents."

"For everything?" Peter asked suspiciously. He knew that couldn't be right. There had to be a catch.

But Crazy Merlin nodded. "All this for a measly nine dollars and ninety-five cents."

"This is more stuff than that guy David Copperfield has!" Bo exclaimed.

"That's why they call me Crazy Merlin," he said. "My prices are insane. Now, do you want it or not?"

"Of course we want it," Peter said, digging into his pocket for cash. He counted out nine dollars and ninety-five cents on the counter.

"How are we supposed to get all this stuff home?" Bo asked.

That was a good question. But before Peter could even begin to worry about it, Crazy Merlin had an answer.

"Just pack everything into the disappearing box," he told them.

"And how are we supposed to get *that* home?" Bo asked. "That thing is huge. It must weigh a ton."

"Not really." Crazy Merlin walked over to the disappearing box. Without any difficulty at all, he lowered it onto the floor so that it was lying on its back with the door on top. "It becomes the Box of Death when you lay it down," he told them. "Now watch this."

There was a button on the side of the box. When Crazy Merlin pushed it, the box began to rise off the floor.

"What's going on?" Peter asked. "More magic?"

"The magic of modern science." Crazy Merlin pointed under the disappearing box. The box was on some kind of platform with wheels. The platform was getting higher and higher. Peter could hear a motor humming away under the box. Crazy Merlin let the disappearing box rise about as high as his waist before he turned off the motor that moved it.

"Now you can wheel it out of here," he told the boys, giving the box a shove in their direction.

Peter collected the other stuff and loaded it into the box as quickly as he could. He didn't want to give Crazy Merlin time to come to his senses and realize that nine ninety-five was too low a price for everything he'd given them.

What Peter didn't know was that he and Bo were going to end up getting a whole lot more than they'd bargained for. And they were going to pay dearly.

9

"We're definitely going to win those bikes with all this stuff Crazy Merlin gave us," Bo said as they wheeled the Starter Kit up Peter's driveway. "Too bad we'll only get to ride them for one day."

"What do you mean?" Peter asked.

"Janitor Bob's going to kill us on Saturday, remember?" Bo reminded him.

Peter hadn't thought about Janitor Bob since they'd gotten home from school. And he didn't want to think about him, either. Not now, anyway. He just wanted to get their Starter Kit into the garage so that he and Bo could start putting together an act.

"Will you just forget about Janitor Bob?" he told Bo. "We'll figure something out."

"Well, you'd better figure it out before Saturday," Bo replied.

"I will," Peter assured him. Then his thoughts turned to something much more pleasant. "How much you want to bet Mary-Margaret Mahoney sets *herself* on fire when she sees our act?"

Bo laughed. "I can't wait to see her start bawling her eyes out when she loses to us."

"And she's going to keep bawling, too," Peter said. "Because I'm going to rub her face in this for the rest of the year."

As Peter slid open the garage door, Grandma Grussler stepped onto the front porch, shaking her box of doggy biscuits and calling for Tiger.

"Tiger," she yelled. "Where are you, you little mouse mangler?"

"What's the matter, Grandma?" Peter called to her.

"Tiger's out mousing again," she answered. "Look." She pointed to a pile of mutilated dead mice by her feet.

"Oh, man." Bo cringed. "That's disgusting."

"If I were smart," she continued, "I would have been saving every one of these mouse bodies over the years."

"For what?" Peter asked.

"For fame and fortune," Grandma Grussler answered. "That cat's killed so many mice, we could have gotten our pictures in *The Guinness Book of World Records*."

"It's true," Peter told Bo.

"Oh, well." She sighed. "It's too late for that now." Grandma Grussler swept the dead mice into a dustpan and headed for the trash can by the garage door.

"Well, well, well," she said after she'd dumped the mice. "What in the world do you boys have here? A coffin?"

Peter laughed. "No, Grandma. It's a magician's box full of magic stuff," he told her. "Bo and I are going to enter the talent contest at school."

"Magic!" she exclaimed. "I love magic. I used to be a magician's assistant, you know."

"Really?" Peter asked.

"Bet your little bippy," she answered, checking out the box. "But I had to give it up when World War Two started. I was too busy flying bomber planes."

"You were a fighter pilot, too?" Bo stifled a laugh.

"Sure was," Grandma Grussler answered. "I'd show you my wings, but I lost them in enemy territory. Let's see what you've got in this box."

Grandma Grussler pulled open the lid and pulled out a sword. "Jumping Jehoshaphat!" she exclaimed. "It's a Blood-Spitting-Gut-Be-Gone sword! I haven't seen one of these since I went on the road with Harry Houdini."

"A what?" Peter asked.

"A Gut-Be-Gone," she repeated, swinging the sword wildly.

"Careful, Grandma," Peter said, jumping out of the way. "Maybe you should just put it back in the box," he suggested. "Before you hurt yourself."

"Nonsense," Grandma Grussler shot back. "I'm an expert at handling Gut-Be-Gones."

Peter sincerely doubted it. Especially when Grandma Grussler swung it over her head and chopped down the plant that was dangling from a hook on the garage ceiling.

"Whoops!" Grandma Grussler exclaimed. "I forgot how sharp the sides of this blade really are. They make them like that so the sword feels real. That way, you can pick a volunteer from the audience to examine the thing."

"Hey, Grandma," Bo piped up. "Maybe you ought to read the instructions first before you chop something else."

"Yeah," Peter whispered. "Like us."

Peter dug through the Starter Kit looking for the instruction booklet. But there wasn't one to be found. Not for any of the stuff.

"Hey, boys," Grandma Grussler exclaimed. "Watch this."

Peter turned to see Grandma Grussler lifting the Gut-Be-Gone over her head as if she were a Samurai warrior. "What are you doing?" he cried.

"Just watch," she said. Then she plunged the Gut-Be-Gone right into her stomach.

Peter and Bo cried out in horror as blood started spurting from Grandma's gut like a fountain.

10

Grandma Grussler fell to the floor with a *thud*, clutching the Gut-Be-Gone. Her eyes were closed, and she wasn't making a sound.

"Grandma!" Peter screamed, falling to his knees beside her. "What have you done?" He watched in shock as the blood continued to spurt.

"Pull the sword out of her!" Bo shrieked.

"I can't!" Peter said. "You do it!"

"She's your grandmother," Bo shouted. "You do it!"

"Oh, pooh," another voice shouted back. "If the two of you are going to fight over me, I'll just take care of it myself."

With that, Grandma Grussler pulled the Gut-Be-Gone from her gut and sprang to her feet.

"Grandma!" Peter cried. "You're not dead!"

"Of course I'm not dead. But I've made a terrible mess of my dress, haven't I?"

Peter and Bo exchanged horrified looks as Grandma Grussler tasted a drop of the blood.

"Thank heavens." She sighed. "This is the good blood. Not that cheap, sticky stuff that stains. Taste a drop," she said, holding out the sword. "It's sweet."

"Oh, man!" Bo gagged as he grabbed his own gut. "I think I'm going to puke!"

Peter gagged, too. "I don't want to taste your blood, Grandma!"

"My blood?" Grandma Grussler laughed. "This isn't my blood. This is fake blood. It's a trick, you silly geese." She chuckled. "I used to do it all the time with Houdini."

"It looked like that sword went right through you," Bo said.

"It's supposed to look that way," Grandma Grussler replied. "But when the tip of the blade hits your stomach, you just push the secret button, and the blade slides right into the handle. See?"

Bo jumped back in a panic as Grandma Grussler touched him with the tip of the sword. The blade retracted.

"Too cool!" Peter exclaimed. "Let me try it!"

"Just make sure you press the button," Grandma Grussler warned Peter. "It's right here on the handle."

Peter pointed the tip of the blade at Bo's stomach. This time, Bo didn't flinch. Sure enough, when Peter hit the button, the blade slid into the handle again.

"Wait a minute," Bo said. "How come there's no blood spraying out of my gut, like you had?" he asked Grandma Grussler.

"The tube inside the sword must be all out of blood," she said. "All you have to do is unscrew the handle and fill it back up again. When the blade collapses, the blood sprays from the top of the handle like crazy. Here. Let me show you." She took the sword from Peter and tried to untwist the handle. "That's funny," Grandma Grussler said, tugging on the handle. "It doesn't come off. It doesn't even twist."

"Let me try," Peter said. But the handle wouldn't budge.

"Aw, man," Bo complained. "We *have* to do this trick in the talent show. But it won't be any good without the blood."

"Maybe we can get the handle off with a wrench or something," Peter suggested.

"You know what?" Grandma Grussler interrupted. "Forget about the stupid sword trick. If you really want to impress your friends, do the Wheel of Torture."

"What's that?" Bo asked.

"This." Grandma Grussler pulled something from the box. It was a collapsible piece of cardboard that opened into a giant circle, just like a spinning wheel. In the center was the shape of a man's body, outlined in white.

"Now this is a really dangerous trick," she told them. She placed the wheel on the huge metal stand she'd also pulled from the box. "Here, let me show you." She handed Peter half a dozen sharp, pointed daggers, then positioned herself in front of the wheel, just like the outlined body. "Now throw those daggers at me, Sonny," she said. "All six of them at once."

Peter and Bo exchanged anxious looks.

"Don't worry," she assured. "They'll collapse like the Gut-Be-Gone."

"Uh, Grandma," Bo gulped. "Aren't there supposed to be fake knives or something that pop up from the back of this thing? I saw a magician on TV talking about this trick once."

"That's right," Peter said, remembering that he'd seen the same show. "The magician said that he doesn't really throw the knife. He just makes believe he's throwing it, then he hides it up his sleeve or something. When the fake knife pops out of the back of the wheel, the audience is tricked into thinking that the magician really did throw it."

"Hmmm." Grandma Grussler's forehead crinkled. "Maybe you're right. I'll tell you what. Maybe we should forget about the Wheel of Torture and try out the Box of Death."

A loud beep stopped Grandma Grussler dead in her tracks. It was the alarm on her cell phone. "Oh, darn." She groaned. "The Box of Death will have to wait. *Global Gladiators* is about to start. The fat lady from Omaha is mud wrestling the pip-squeak from Poughkeepsie today. I can't wait to see her get creamed."

With that, Grandma Grussler raced into the house.

"No way Grandma Grussler watches *Global Gladiators!*" Bo laughed.

"She watches roller derby, too," Peter said.

"My grandmother only watches soap operas," Bo said. "She's nowhere near as cool as Grandma Grussler. But then again, she's nowhere near as nuts, either."

Peter laughed.

"Hey, you don't think Grandma Grussler really flew fighter planes in World War Two, do you?" Bo asked.

"I doubt it," Peter said. "And I don't think she was Harry Houdini's assistant, either. There's no way she's that old."

"So how'd she know how the sword worked?" Bo asked.

"Who knows." Peter shrugged. "But check out these daggers. They definitely don't collapse. There are no fake knives on the Wheel of Torture, either. She really would have gotten stabbed if I'd thrown the daggers at her."

"The Wheel of Torture is definitely out," Bo said.

Peter agreed. It was just too dangerous. "Let's try the Box of Death," he suggested. He emptied the other magic tricks out of the box and piled them onto the floor. "Get in," he told Bo. "I'll stick you with the swords."

"No way," Bo shot back. "You get in."

"I'm the magician," Peter said. "The magician always gets to stab the assistant."

"Not with these swords," Bo said, picking one up off the floor.

"They won't hurt you," Peter told him. "They re-tract." He hit the button on the handle to prove it. But the blade didn't collapse.

Bo threw him a look.

"Maybe these swords work differently," Peter said. "Maybe you have to slide them through the holes in the box before they'll retract."

"I'm not getting in that box," Bo said.

"Then how are we going to try this trick?" Peter asked. Suddenly he had an idea. "I know," he said. "We'll put Blow-up Man in the box and try it on him."

"Who's Blow-up Man?" Bo asked.

"The blow-up doll my mom got when she took that CPR class at the Y," Peter told him. "Remember?"

Bo grinned. "Good idea. Let's stab Blow-up Man."

Within three minutes flat, Blow-up Man was blown up and inside the box.

"Close the lid," Peter told Bo. "You'll see what a baby you're being."

As soon as the lid was down, Peter slid the first sword into the side of the box. He could feel the tip of the blade touch the side of Blow-up Man's body.

"Now watch," he told Bo. "It's going to retract, just like the Gut-Be-Gone."

But as Peter hit the button on the handle, the tip of the blade shot right through the other side of the box. Inside the box, where Bo would have been lying, Blow-up Man exploded with a horrible *pop*.

11

Peter lifted the lid of the box. Blow-up Man was history.

"Get yourself another assistant," Bo snapped. "There's no way I'm risking my life to win some stupid talent show."

"Stop being such a wimp," Peter grumbled. "You're not going to risk your life."

"You just killed Blow-up Man!" Bo shot back. "If I'd been in that box, you would have killed *me*!"

"He only popped because he's a balloon guy," Peter said. "I guarantee you it works differently on people." He pulled the sword from the box and fiddled with the handle. The blade still didn't retract.

"You can guarantee me all you want." Bo folded his arms. "I'm not getting in that box. And I'm not doing any more sword tricks with you, either. So you're just going to have to get in that box and stick yourself." Bo headed for the door.

"Come on," Peter pleaded. "You've got to help me. I promise we won't do any dangerous tricks."

"Forget it," Bo said. "Without the big tricks, we'll be even worse than Gerald MacDougal. There's no way I'm getting up on that stage so that everybody in school can laugh at me. Especially if I'm just the assistant."

"I'll let you wear the magic amulet," Peter offered. He picked it up and held it out to Bo.

"Get that thing away from me." Bo hit Peter's arm, and the amulet went flying. "I'm not wearing a necklace! And I'm not being your assistant!"

Just then Tiger walked into the garage. The cat jumped into the disappearing box, which was still lying on its side.

"You want an assistant?" Bo went on. "There." He slammed the lid of the disappearing box. "The stupid cat can be your assistant."

"Very funny," Peter muttered. Then he lifted the lid to free Tiger.

But Tiger didn't jump out.

"Come on, Tiger," Peter hollered impatiently. "Get out of there!"

The cat still didn't come out.

Peter groaned as he bent over to look inside the box. "He's gone!" Peter gasped. "Tiger's disappeared!"

"No, sir," Bo said. Then he looked for himself. "I can't believe it! The stupid cat figured out how to make the disappearing box work. Now we've got a trick!"

"Too cool," Peter said. "All we've got to do is figure out where he went. Tiger?" Peter thumped on the bottom of the box.

No Tiger.

Bo looked under the box. No Tiger. "You don't think he really disappeared, do you?"

"Of course not!" Peter laughed.

"What if he did?" Bo said. "What if this stuff really is magic, like Crazy Merlin said?"

"I wish," Peter said, picking up the magic wand. "Then we wouldn't have to worry about trying to figure out these tricks. I could just wave this magic wand and say 'Abracadabra, make Tiger appear.'"

A beam of light shot out from the prism on the end of the stick. It hit the disappearing box with a crackle of electricity.

Peter was so startled, he jumped back and dropped the wand on the floor. "What was that?" he cried.

"I don't know." Bo blinked his eyes. "That wand just shot a laser or something. Maybe it really does work."

No way, Peter told himself. That would be too good to be true. But before he could answer Bo, he heard something.

"Meow!"

"Did you hear that?" Peter asked Bo.

"Meow!" They heard the sound again. It was coming from inside the disappearing box.

"Tiger?" Peter moved toward the box. He didn't dare let himself believe that it was true, that he really had performed magic. If Tiger was inside the box, it was only because he'd climbed out of the secret compartment where he'd been hiding.

But Peter was wrong. He knew it the moment he threw open the lid of the box.

He really had performed magic. Because the tiger inside the box was not the cat he'd expected to see.

It was a tiger! A *real* tiger, with fangs as long and as sharp as the swords.

12

P eter and Bo stood frozen in terror.

The tiger in the box was just as still. It sat there staring at Peter with its big yellow cat eyes, licking its drooling chops.

"Do something," Bo squeaked.

Peter swallowed hard. Then he reached out quickly and slammed the lid of the box shut.

"I can't believe you turned Tiger into a tiger!" Bo's voice rose with his panic.

Peter couldn't believe it, either. He just hoped he could turn the tiger back into *Tiger*. He snatched up the magic wand and waved it at the box furiously.

"Abracadabra and all that junk," he cried. "Please, please, please, shrink Tiger back into a house cat!"

"Nothing happened!" Bo shrieked.

"Come on, you stupid thing," Peter said, slapping the wand against his hand. "Work!" He pointed it back at the box. "Abracadabra," he commanded. "Turn Tiger back into a cat!"

"*Me-oooooow.*" The sound drifted out of the box.

Peter and Bo exchanged looks.

"He *sounds* normal," Bo whispered.

"He sounded that way before, too," Peter reminded him.

"Maybe we ought to check," Bo suggested.

"No way I'm opening that box again!" Peter told him.

But the box opened anyway. Tiger—the *big* tiger— was pushing up the lid with its enormous striped head.

Peter and Bo began backing away. But before they could turn and run, the tiger sprang out of the box. It landed inches away from Peter. Now they were nose to nose. Peter could feel the cat's hot breath as the tiger opened its mouth.

Peter opened his mouth, too—to scream! He was sure he was about to be eaten.

But instead of sinking its fangs into Peter, the tiger licked him in the face with its huge, sandpaper tongue. Then it rubbed its head against Peter, the same way Tiger the cat used to do. But this cat was so big, it almost knocked Peter over.

"Tiger?" Peter said to the cat. "Is that really you?"

Tiger lay down on the floor and rolled over, purring like an engine.

"It *is* Tiger," Bo cried. "Look, he's still wearing his collar. It really is Grandma Grussler's cat, just a whole lot bigger."

"Well, we'd better figure out how to make him smaller again," Peter said, patting Tiger's stomach. "If Grandma Grussler sees him like this, she'll freak."

Peter spent the next ten minutes waving the magic wand at Tiger. But he didn't shrink an inch.

"It's not working," Bo said, pointing out the obvious. "Maybe it's all used up, just like that Gut-Be-Gone sword."

"How can it be all used up?" Peter turned his frustration on Bo. "There was nothing in it to start with."

But Peter was wrong. The magic wand was made up of two pieces screwed tightly together. Maybe there was something inside. Peter took the wand apart to find out.

"Batteries!" he exclaimed, shocked at what he found. "Is it possible that this magic wand works on batteries?"

"Who knows?" Bo shrugged. "Up until a few minutes ago, I didn't think it was possible that it would work at all."

Peter dumped the two batteries from the wand into his hand. They were rusted and much thinner than any battery Peter had ever seen before.

"What kind are they?" Bo asked.

"I can't tell," Peter answered. If there had been a brand name on the cells, it was long gone.

"Well, we'd better get some new ones," Bo said.

"Where are we going to find batteries like this?" Peter wondered.

Bo had the answer. "At the hardware store in town. They have everything."

There was only one problem. "The hardware store

closes at five o'clock," Peter told Bo. "It's way past that now. We're going to have to wait until tomorrow."

"Tomorrow!" Bo said. "What the heck are you going to do with him until then?" He pointed at Tiger, who was still purring at Peter's feet.

"I guess I'm going to have to hide him," Peter said.

Now that was definitely going to be a trick.

13

"What did you do with the cat?" Bo whispered to Peter as he slid into his seat. Bo crammed his books under his desk. The first bell of the day had already signaled the start of classes, and Bo was two and a half minutes late. Luckily, their teacher hadn't arrived yet.

"Where were you this morning?" Peter asked. "I texted you but you didn't answer. I thought you were going to meet me at the bus stop."

"I overslept," Bo answered. "My mom had to drive me to school. She was pretty angry about it."

"I can't believe you," Peter grumbled. "*I'm* having a nervous breakdown all night, and you overslept."

"I was tired," Bo said.

"From what?" Peter demanded. "I'm the one who had to deal with Tiger all night."

"Was it my fault I had to go home for dinner?" Bo shot back.

"Well, I haven't had any sleep," Peter complained.

"So what did you do with the cat?" Bo asked again.

"I chained him up in the garage," Peter answered. "Grandma Grussler thinks he's still out mousing."

"Are you nuts?" Bo said. "What if he gets loose?"

"He's not going to get loose," Peter replied. "I hooked the chain to his collar and wrapped it around the leg of my father's tool cabinet. That tool cabinet weighs a ton. And the chain is like ten inches thick."

Bo shook his head. "I still think you made a mistake," he said.

"What did you want me to do?" Peter barked. "Hide him under my bed?"

"I just hope he doesn't get out," Bo said.

"What's he going to do?" Peter sneered. "Press the automatic door opener?"

"He's a tiger," Bo said. "If he wanted to, he could

probably break down the door. I hope you fed him a big breakfast this morning," he went on. "Who knows what'll happen if that cat gets hungry."

Peter's heart skipped a beat. He'd been so worried about hiding Tiger, he'd never thought about feeding him.

"You did feed him, didn't you?" Bo asked.

Peter shook his head.

"Oh, man," Bo cried. "He's probably starving. And if he does get out, he's going to go hunting for something a whole lot bigger than mice—like zebras."

Peter swallowed hard. "That's not going to happen," he snapped. "Besides, there aren't any zebras around here!"

"There are at the zoo, which is less than twenty miles from here," Bo informed him. "And guess what, pal? Tigers can run like *sixty* miles an hour."

"Just shut up already, okay?" Peter shouted.

So did Mr. Sherman, their teacher. "Mr. Newman!" he barked as he entered the classroom and headed for his desk. "What is the rule in this classroom once the bell rings?"

"Silence?" Peter gulped.

"Whether I'm here or not," Mr. Sherman added.

"Sorry," Peter apologized.

But the teacher pulled out a pink slip anyway. "Talking after the bell gets you one demerit," he said.

Terrific, Peter thought. This was already turning into a disastrous day, and he still had a hungry Tiger waiting for him at home.

By the time the last bell of the day rang, Peter was so jittery, he felt like he had butt-biting ants in his pants. He couldn't get out of the school building fast enough.

He and Bo had to go to the hardware store before they headed home. Their only hope of changing the zebra-eating tiger back into a mouse-eating cat was to find some new batteries for the magic wand.

But the hardware store didn't have any batteries that would fit the wand. In fact, the hardware salesman told Peter that the batteries from the wand were more than sixty years old. No one even made them anymore. The best the hardware guy could do was try to recharge the old ones.

"I sure hope these batteries work," Bo said as they headed toward Peter's driveway.

"Tell me about it," Peter said, clutching the rusted cells in his hand.

Just then, Peter heard someone calling his name. It was Mrs. Foxworthy, his neighbor.

"Peter," she said, heading toward them. She was carrying a dog leash, and she looked upset. "Have either of you seen Boxer?"

Boxer was Mrs. Foxworthy's dog.

Peter and Bo shook their heads.

"We were taking a walk," she continued. "I let Boxer off this leash so he could run a bit, but when I turned my back, he disappeared. He's done this before." Mrs. Foxworthy sighed. "But this time I'm really worried."

"Why?" Peter asked nervously.

"I thought I heard Boxer yelping back in the woods," she explained, "but I couldn't find him anywhere."

Bo shot Peter a look. "Boxer's a Great Dane, right?"

Mrs. Foxworthy nodded.

"And he's just about the size of a zebra, isn't he?"

Now Peter shot Bo a look.

"Not quite," Mrs. Foxworthy answered. "But he's a very big dog. If you see him, will you please let me know?"

"Sure thing, Mrs. Foxworthy," Peter said. He and Bo took off up the driveway in a panic. Peter was half expecting to see Boxer lying on his front porch on top of a pile of other neighborhood dogs. But the front porch was totally clear.

The problem was, so was the garage.

Peter let out a scream as he opened the door.

Tiger's collar was still hooked to the chain. And the chain was still hooked to the cabinet. But Tiger was gone.

14

I knew it." Bo buried his face in his hands. "I knew this was a bad idea."

Peter lifted Tiger's collar from the floor. "How the heck did he get out of this collar?" he wondered.

"Who knows." Bo moaned. "But he must have pushed the automatic opener to get out of the garage," he said. "Because he didn't break down the door."

"We have to find him," Peter said. "We have to search the neighborhood."

"No way," Bo declared. "I'm not searching for that cat."

"Why not?" Peter asked.

"Because I don't want to find him," Bo said. "He just ate a Great Dane! And with our luck, he's still hungry."

"We don't know that for sure," Peter told him.

"Cut me a break," Bo huffed. "Tiger's missing, and so is Mrs. Foxworthy's zebra-sized dog. You don't have to be a rocket scientist to put two and two together."

"We can't just let Tiger roam around the neighborhood," Peter pointed out.

"Yes, we can," Bo insisted. "Let's just hope there's another Great Dane roaming it with him. Otherwise he'll start eating kids!"

Bo was working Peter into such a frenzy, Peter couldn't think straight. "Come on," he said, tugging Bo's arm. "I'm going to call the police."

"Oh, no, you're not." Bo tugged back. "No way I'm going to prison for this."

"For what?" Peter snapped.

"For setting a tiger loose on the public," Bo answered.

"We didn't set him loose," Peter said. "He ran away."

"Well, something tells me it's against the law to keep

a tiger in your house," he shot back. "Besides, what are you going to say when the police ask you where he came from? A magic wand?"

Bo had a point. He also had an idea.

"I know," he told Peter. "We can call the animal control people and tell them we saw one of the tigers break loose from the zoo. We'll say he was heading in this direction. They'll send somebody out here to shoot him with a tranquilizer dart so they can take him back to the zoo. Then, if the batteries work again, we can take the magic wand out to the zoo and turn Tiger back into a cat. That way, we won't get ourselves arrested—or killed."

"What if we get arrested for lying to the animal control people?" Peter asked.

"We won't," Bo assured him. "We'll call them anonymously."

It was a crazy idea. But Peter was desperate. If Tiger really was eating neighborhood pets, somebody had to stop him fast.

"Fine," Peter said. "But you're calling. We'll use Grandma Grussler's phone. That way, they can't trace the call back to us."

"Good idea," Bo agreed.

Peter and Bo headed for the back door so Grandma Grussler wouldn't hear them come in.

Peter pushed the door open slowly so that it wouldn't make a sound. But the second he stepped through it, *he* made a sound. In fact, he gasped so loudly, Bo let out a scream.

Sitting in the middle of the laundry room floor was Tiger's litter box. In the center of it was a mountain of cat poop. *Big* cat poop, the size of the tiger's!

"He's in the house!" Peter cried. "Tiger's in the house!"

"Oh man." Bo cringed as he stared at the litter box. "*That* must be the Great Dane."

Peter tore through the laundry room into the kitchen. There he was greeted by another horrifying sight—Grandma Grussler's chewed-up slippers. They were sitting in a puddle of milk on the floor. On the counter, an open milk carton was lying on its side, still dripping.

"Holy smokes!" Bo gasped. "He ate Grandma Grussler—and washed her down with milk!"

Peter was thinking the very same thing. "Grandma!"

he cried, racing into the living room. "Grandma, where are you?"

The TV was on, but the rocker was empty.

Peter's heart was pumping so fast, he thought he was going to pass out—until Grandma Grussler appeared from the bathroom.

"What's all the screaming about?" she asked.

"Grandma, you're alive!"

"And kicking," she added, sitting down in her rocker. "Why?"

"No reason," Peter lied. "Just checking."

"Ask her if she's seen Tiger," Bo whispered.

"Uh, Grandma," Peter fumbled. "By any chance, have you seen Tiger today?"

"He's in this house somewhere," she said. "He must have snuck back in when I went out for the mail this morning."

"Have you seen him?" Bo repeated Peter's question.

"No," Grandma Grussler answered. "He's been hiding from me all day because he knows I'm going to yell at him for staying out all night. He's probably as hungry as a lion by now," she said. "So he's going to have to show his face sooner or later."

Tiger's not as hungry as a lion, Peter thought. *He's as hungry as a tiger! And trust me, Grandma, you don't want him to show his face.*

But a few seconds later, Tiger *did* show his face.

"Meow. Me-oooooow . . ."

Peter heard the cries first. They were coming from the top of the stairs that led to the family room. And they were getting closer by the second. Tiger was on his way down!

Bo ran for the door in a panic.

Just as Peter was about to grab Grandma Grussler from her rocker and drag her to the door, too, Tiger leapt to the landing.

Peter gasped when he saw the cat's face. It wasn't the face he expected—the face of a starving, Great Dane–swallowing beast. It was the face of a cat—a small cat.

Peter stood staring at the cat, his mouth hanging open in shock. Tiger wasn't a tiger anymore—and they hadn't even tried the recharged magic wand.

15

I don't want to do this," Bo complained. It was Thursday afternoon, the last day of auditions, and they were standing backstage in the school auditorium waiting for their turn.

"All we have to do is fake our way through this audition today," Peter said. "Only nine other acts have tried out today. As long as the judges see that we have some kind of talent, they'll let us in the show. We can come up with some better tricks tonight so we can win tomorrow."

"It's never going to happen." Bo continued to moan.

"We practiced all *last* night, and we still don't have an act!"

Peter knew Bo was right. They had a couple of tricks, but not an act, not really.

They'd tried like crazy to do something spectacular like changing Tiger the cat into something safe, like Tiger the mouse. But even with the batteries recharged, the magic wand didn't work. Bo refused to try any of the dangerous tricks. And Peter couldn't even get the stupid handkerchief trick to work the right way.

All they were left with were a couple of card tricks, the bone-crunching handcuffs, and a really gross lip-sewing trick that they couldn't get right. For nine ninety-five, this magic act was a total dud.

But Peter refused to admit defeat.

"I'm telling you," he told Bo. "We'll get through this audition just fine."

"What's the point?" Bo griped. "We're never going to win tomorrow. It's hopeless." Bo didn't let up. "If you need proof, just look at Stanley Weiner."

Stanley Weiner was onstage, in the middle of his

audition. As luck would have it, he was doing a magic act, too—a good one.

Peter watched in horror as "Stan the Man" went through his act.

First, he pulled a bunch of flowers out of his magic wand. He handed them to Mrs. Dingleman, who giggled as she took them.

"Kiss-up," Peter muttered under his breath.

Next, Stanley began to pull an endless stream of colorful scarves from his assistant's ear.

"This is terrible," Bo said as the judges applauded.

It *was* terrible—for Peter and Bo.

Stanley's tricks got better and better. He made a cone out of a sheet of newspaper. Then his assistant, Wendy, poured a pitcher of water into the cone.

The judges ducked when Stanley shook out the paper in their direction.

Peter hoped they would all be splashed, but he was sorely disappointed. There was no water anywhere. Stanley's newspaper was dry as a bone.

When Stanley took Mrs. Dingleman's watch, wrapped it in a handkerchief, and began to smash it with a hammer, Peter was sure that Stanley had gone too far. He couldn't wait to see Mrs. Dingleman's face when Stanley gave back her watch in pieces.

But Stanley was still smiling as he shook the handkerchief so the audience could hear the shattered watch jingling. Mrs. Dingleman looked none too happy. Until Stanley threw open the handkerchief and returned her watch, good as new.

The judges applauded enthusiastically. But nowhere near as enthusiastically as they did for Stanley's grand finale, when he pulled a white dove out of his top hat.

"Stanley Weiner is going to win the talent show," Bo told Peter. "Even Mary-Margaret Mahoney doesn't stand a chance next to him. I say we get out of here while we still can."

Peter might have been persuaded if there had been more time. But it was too late to run.

"Next up is another magic act," Mrs. Dingleman said. "Peter Newman and Bo Wilson." She called them onto the stage.

The judges applauded politely as Peter and Bo took their places. But Peter could tell by the looks on their faces that they didn't have high hopes, especially after Stanley's performance.

"Well, gentlemen, what are you going to show us today?" Mrs. Dingleman asked.

"First, some card tricks," Peter said, trying to sound as if he knew what he was doing. "I have here a brand-new deck of cards." He produced them from his pocket.

The deck looked brand-new. But it wasn't. That was the real trick. The box was resealable so that it looked as though it had never been opened before. The other trick was that all fifty-two cards in the deck were the ace of spades.

"My assistant will shuffle the deck." Peter took the cards out of the pack and handed them to Bo. "Then a member of the audience will be asked to pick a card. And using my magic power, I will be able to tell you which card it is."

Bo shuffled the cards. But when he tried to get fancy about it, the cards flew out of his hands and fluttered to the floor all over the stage.

Peter hit Bo in the stomach with his magic wand. "You idiot," he snarled as the audience laughed.

Peter had to find a way to save face. Luckily, an idea popped into his head.

"For making that unforgivable mistake," Peter shouted over the laughter, "I will now handcuff my assistant." He pulled the handcuffs out of his other pocket. "Hands behind your back," he instructed Bo.

Bo played along, doing as he was told.

Peter snapped the cuffs on him.

"Ouch," Bo hollered. "That hurts."

"Serves you right," Peter said under his breath. But to the audience he said, "Should I let him go?"

Nobody answered. Finally Mrs. Dingleman piped up. "Yes," she said. "Let him go."

"All right," Peter said. "I will free him by magic." He waved the wand at Bo. "Abracadabra. You're free."

Bo yanked at the handcuffs. But they held fast.

Peter tried again. "Abracadabra. You're free." Then he whispered, "Just pull them apart, the way we practiced."

"I'm trying," Bo said. "But it's not working."

The audience began to laugh again.

"Open them with the key," Bo said loud enough for everyone to hear. "This is stupid. I quit!"

"I don't think so," Peter said, determined to go on, no matter what. "But I sure am tired of listening to your complaining. So now I'm going to shut you up for good."

Peter pulled a long, sharp needle out of his pocket. It was threaded with thick, black thread.

"Oh, no," Bo said, backing away. His eyes were just about popping out of his head in terror.

Peter knew that with his hands cuffed behind his back, there was nothing Bo could do to defend himself.

"Oh, yes," Peter said. "Now I'm going to sew your lips shut."

"Noooooooo!" Bo screamed.

But before he'd even finished, Peter had stuck the needle right through Bo's bottom lip.

16

"Peter Newman!" Mrs. Dingleman shrieked. "You stop that right now!"

Peter wasn't about to stop—not when he'd finally found a trick that had the audience's attention. He could hear the horrified gasps filling the auditorium.

"Scream louder," Peter whispered to Bo as he stuck the needle through Bo's upper lip.

Bo let out a wail.

"Peter Newman!" Mrs. Dingleman rose from her seat. "I said stop that!"

But Peter kept right on sewing. He pulled the thread

through Bo's upper lip and gave it a good, hard tug, forcing Bo's two lips together.

Bo tried to open his mouth to scream again. That was a big mistake. His lips fell right off his face and landed *splat* on the floor at his feet.

"Oh, no," Peter groaned in disgust. The trick had gone horribly wrong. He just hoped he could do something to save it before the audience caught on. "Quick," he told Bo. "Bite down on the blood capsule."

"I can't," Bo muttered. "I swallowed it."

It was too late anyway. The illusion was over. The audience was already starting to snicker. And Bo didn't make things any better when he finally wriggled out of his handcuffs and bent down to pick up his fake lips.

Even Mrs. Dingleman was roaring with laughter. "I think your act needs a little work," she told Peter, wiping tears from her eyes. "Unless it's meant to be a comedy act."

"No," Peter told her, sounding as insulted as he felt. "It's a magic act. And it'll be great by tomorrow. You'll see. You'll all be surprised." With that he turned and headed off the stage with Bo right behind him.

"Mary-Margaret Mahoney and Carol Ann Finster," Mrs. Dingleman called.

"Hey, wait a minute," Peter said as he watched Mary-Margaret and Carol Ann take the stage. "How come Mary-Margaret gets to audition twice?"

"Because Mary-Margaret is multitalented," Mrs. Dingleman explained. "And because Carol Ann can't very well sing a duet by herself, can she?"

"Carol Ann can't sing at all," Peter said. "Neither can Mary-Margaret, for that matter."

Bo snickered at the comment. But he was the only one.

"Look who's talking," Mary-Margaret taunted. "You have some nerve entering a talent competition when you don't even have any talent."

Now everybody snickered.

"I hate her," Peter growled at Bo as he stormed away from Mary-Margaret. He stomped down the steps on the side of the stage and headed up the aisle.

Then Mary-Margaret and Carol Ann began to sing, and Peter couldn't help turning around to get a look at them.

Bo covered his ears and was grimacing as if he were in terrible pain. Peter did the same thing, making sure that Mary-Margaret saw him. He hoped it would psych her out and make her mess up her song.

But Mary-Margaret didn't miss a note. She went right on singing with a smug look on her face.

That just made Peter even angrier. He wished more than anything that he could wipe that smile off her face.

"Abracadabra." Peter waved his magic wand at Mary-Margaret. "Shut her up."

Zap!

A shock shot up Peter's arm. It stunned him so badly, he opened his hand and dropped the magic wand.

He could still feel the tingling in the finger the magician's ring was on. He held his hand in front of his face and saw that the ring had changed. The stone had turned from blue to jet black.

Peter nudged Bo to show him what had happened. But Bo's eyes were fixed on the stage. "Something's wrong with Mary-Margaret," he whispered.

Peter looked up. He saw that Mary-Margaret's lips were moving, but no sound was coming out of her mouth.

Carol Ann continued singing at the top of her lungs. Her "solo" filled the auditorium.

"Mary-Margaret?" Mrs. Dingleman cried as Mary-Margaret grabbed her throat with a look of utter terror on her face. "Mary-Margaret," Mrs. Dingleman repeated. "What's the matter?" In a flash, Mrs. Dingleman darted onto the stage to help her stricken student.

Meanwhile, Peter bent down to pick up the magic wand.

"What did you do to Mary-Margaret?" Bo asked Peter.

Peter had no idea. But one thing was certain. The magic wand had worked again.

17

Somebody get the nurse!" Mrs. Dingleman shouted.

Mary-Margaret fell to her knees, still clutching her throat. It seemed as though the more attention she got, the more she carried on. Suddenly, she was acting as if she were going to die.

"Maybe we should call nine-one-one," another teacher shouted. It was the same teacher who'd pulled the fire alarm on Monday.

If Peter weren't so freaked out by what he'd just done, he probably would have laughed.

Bo *was* laughing. "Aw, man," he whispered to Peter. "This is too cool. You shut Mary-Margaret up for good."

Peter couldn't believe it. It was like a dream come true. Too bad he couldn't tell anyone—he'd probably get a medal.

Up on stage, Mary-Margaret continued her theatrics, surrounded by teachers and the nurse.

"I'm going to call your mother, dear," the nurse said to Mary-Margaret. "I think you should see your doctor right away."

Mary-Margaret started screaming hysterically—but no sound came out.

"What in the world is going on here?" a loud voice boomed as Janitor Bob suddenly appeared out of nowhere.

"Uh-oh," Bo said. "Look who's here."

Peter's heart stopped.

"Mary-Margaret's lost her voice," the nurse told Janitor Bob. "One minute she was singing, and the next minute she went totally mute. Her throat's not red. And she doesn't have a fever. I've never seen anything like this."

Janitor Bob glared out into the auditorium. Peter could practically feel his gaze burning a hole through the seat they were hiding behind.

"Trust me, I know how to fix this," Janitor Bob said, turning his attention back to Mary-Margaret. He reached into his pocket and pulled out a box of lozenges. "Just suck on one of these." He dropped one into her hand. "They're cherry flavored, and sweeter than candy."

Mary-Margaret popped the lozenge into her mouth. A second later, her obnoxious, shrill voice filled the auditorium.

"I'm all better!" she shrieked.

The nurse was stunned. So was everyone else.

"I think I can even sing now," Mary-Margaret continued. "Listen," she said. Then she opened her mouth and let out a note nearly as high-pitched as a dog whistle.

"Maybe you ought to rest your throat a bit, dear," Mrs. Dingleman said.

"Don't worry," Janitor Bob interrupted. "She's just fine. You can let her sing her little heart out."

"The show must go on," Mary-Margaret told Mrs. Dingleman.

"Oh, puke," Bo whispered to Peter. "Let's get out of here."

Peter and Bo sneaked down the aisle, ducking down as low as the seats as they headed toward the back door of the auditorium. But they'd taken only a few steps when they were stopped dead in their tracks.

"Freeze right where you are," Janitor Bob ordered. He moved in front of them. "I saw what you did. And I didn't like it one bit."

Peter felt the blood draining from his face.

"You're going to pay for this crime on Saturday morning," Janitor Bob warned them. "That's right." He chuckled. "On Saturday morning, I'm going to make the *two of you* sing like canaries."

18

"Will you stop worrying about the stupid talent show and start worrying about Janitor Bob?" Bo fumed. Bo had been doing nothing *but* worrying about Janitor Bob since he'd thrown them out of the auditorium by the backs of their shirt collars.

"I just wish we could get this stupid wand to work again," Peter complained, trying to do just that.

But no matter how hard he waved the wand, or how loudly he said "abracadabra," he still couldn't turn the squirrel he saw into a bird, or the bird he saw into an airplane. He couldn't even change the red light at the corner green so that he and Bo could cross the street without waiting.

Bo sighed. "Too bad we can't wave the wand at Janitor Bob and make *him* sing like a canary."

"He's not really going to make us sing, you know," Peter informed Bo. "It's just an expression."

"For what?" Bo asked.

"For torture."

Bo went pale. "You're kidding me, right?"

Peter shook his head.

"He's going to torture us first and *then* kill us?" Bo gulped.

"Probably," Peter confirmed.

"Give me that thing," Bo said, grabbing the wand. "Work, you stupid stick! We have to get rid of Janitor Bob!" He shook the wand furiously, but still nothing happened.

"I just don't get it," Peter said. "There has to be a reason why this stupid wand works sometimes and not others."

"Maybe the batteries need to be recharged again," Bo suggested.

Peter shook his head. "If it were just the batteries, the wand would have worked yesterday when we tried to turn Tiger into a mouse," he told Bo. "But it didn't work at all until I waved it at Mary-Margaret."

"Maybe it didn't work on Mary-Margaret, either," Bo said. "Maybe it was just a coincidence. I mean, the wand didn't shoot a laser or anything when you waved it at her."

"Well, it must have shot some kind of electricity," Peter said. "Because this ring zapped me, too. And look," he told Bo, holding out his hand. "The stone is blue again."

"So?" Bo said.

"*Sooooo*, something weird must have happened," Peter replied. He tugged at the ring to get it off. But it wouldn't budge.

Bo waved the wand at Peter. "Yeah, well, nothing weird's happening now," he said.

"We're just going to have to forget about the wand and figure out something else we can use," Peter said.

"How many times do I have to tell you?" Bo snapped. "I'm not doing the stupid talent show! I'm not going to spend my last day on earth being humiliated."

"You're not going to be humiliated," Peter said. "Not if we do the Box of Death trick."

"Are you out of your mind?" Bo said. "What do you want to do? Kill me tomorrow afternoon before Janitor Bob gets to do it on Saturday morning?"

"I won't kill you," Peter assured him.

"Tell that to Blow-up Man," Bo shot back.

"Blow-up Man was a balloon," Peter said. "I'll bet if we put something solid in that box, the swords would retract the way they're supposed to."

"Forget it," Bo said.

"What if I get in first?" Peter said. "Will you do it then?"

Bo thought about it as they entered Peter's garage. Then he made up his mind. "Get in," he told Peter.

Peter climbed into the box. As he lay down, he stuck his feet out through the foot holes and his arms out through the arm holes. His head poked out the top.

"I'm not closing the lid," Bo said, picking up one of the swords. "If this sword doesn't retract, I want to make sure I don't push it all the way through you."

"Fine," Peter told him. "Just make sure you hit the

button on the handle when the sword touches my body."

Peter held his breath as Bo slid the first sword into the box. He watched the blade moving closer and closer. The point of the sword grazed his skin. But it didn't go through him.

"It worked!" Bo exclaimed as the sword retracted.

"I told you it would," Peter said.

Bo made Peter stay in the box until he'd tried every sword. When he was certain they all worked, Peter climbed out, and Bo climbed in. He even let Peter close the lid so they could practice the trick the way they'd do it onstage.

"Ready?" Peter asked Bo.

Bo nodded.

Peter slid the first sword into the box. He felt the tip of the blade touch Bo's body. Then he pressed the button to retract the blade.

"Are you okay?" he asked Bo.

"Yup," Bo answered, "I didn't feel a thing."

Peter slid the next sword through, just as slowly, with exactly the same results.

Bo smiled. "With this trick, we'll definitely make 'Stan the Man' look like a weenie magician."

Peter laughed. Bo was finally getting into it.

With each sword, Peter grew more and more sure of himself. He was sliding the blades through much more quickly now. By the time he picked up the last sword, he felt totally confident.

"Now I will pierce my assistant's heart," he proclaimed, pretending to be onstage.

"Noooooo!" Bo cried dramatically, following Peter's lead. "Don't let me die!"

As Peter plunged the sword through the box, Bo let out another bloodcurdling scream. "Stop it!" he shrieked.

"Great acting job!" Peter laughed.

Bo kept on screaming.

And Peter kept on laughing—until he saw the blood gushing up from the sword hole in the box.

19

Peter's heart leapt to his throat as the blood squirting up from the box splattered onto his face. Blow-up Man wasn't the only thing that had exploded in that box—so had Bo's heart!

"Help!" Peter started to scream. "Somebody help me! I just killed my best friend!" He was about to run for the door when Bo started to laugh.

"Gotcha!" Bo said.

"What do you mean, 'gotcha'?" Peter cried. "I just got *you*! In case you haven't noticed, you're bleeding to death. I just stabbed you through the heart!"

"No sir." Bo kept laughing. "I squirted some blood

capsules through the hole to make it look real! Open the box and I'll show you."

"I can't believe you did that." Peter sighed, doubling over to catch his breath. "You almost gave me a heart attack. I feel like throwing up!"

Bo smiled devilishly. "Yeah, well, if I scared you, just imagine what we'll do to the crowd tomorrow."

Peter smiled, too.

Thanks to Bo's Academy Award–winning performance and a handful of blood capsules, they finally had an act—one they spent the next several hours perfecting.

By the time the following afternoon rolled around, Peter and Bo were all set for the show. Unfortunately, they had no way of knowing that the Box of Death was going to slay more than the audience.

20

Peter could feel his adrenaline pumping as he and Bo stood backstage watching Mary-Margaret Mahoney take her final bow. At least he hoped it was her final bow. She'd already taken three of them, even though the audience had stopped clapping a bow and a half ago.

Without the fire baton, Mary-Margaret's hoedown routine was dull. Everybody knew it. Peter felt pretty confident that her duet with Carol Ann would be even worse, and just as easy to beat. And while Stan the Man had gotten a couple of "oohs" and "aahs" from the crowd with his magic act, Peter was sure he and Bo would get a standing ovation—if only they could get out on stage.

"Hey, Mary-Margaret," Bo shouted from behind the curtains. "Get off the stage already, will you? Nobody's clapping!"

Peter cracked up as Mary-Margaret took another final, final bow, then headed off the stage at last. "I hope you *really* break a leg out there," she snapped as she stormed past them.

Out in the auditorium, Mrs. Dingleman rose to announce the next act. "Up next," she said, scanning her list, "we have Peter the Great and his Little Magic Act of Horrors."

"Great name," Bo whispered as he started to wheel the Box of Death onto the stage.

"I thought it up this morning," Peter said, dragging the bag of swords behind him. "Pretty cool, huh?"

"Beats 'Gerald MacDougal and his Magnificent McPipes.'" Bo laughed.

So did Peter and half of the audience as he and Bo took center stage—the half of the audience who had watched their audition.

"Oh, brother," a voice called from the crowd. "What are you guys going to do now? Sew your butts together?"

The crowd roared.

"One more remark like that and every one of you will be spending Monday afternoon in detention," Mrs. Dingleman barked.

Silence fell in the auditorium as Mrs. Dingleman turned back to the boys. "I'd better not see anything rude up on that stage," she told Peter and Bo under her breath.

"You won't, Mrs. Dingleman," Peter assured her. "But it is going to be kind of gory," he warned her.

Mrs. Dingleman rolled her eyes. Then she plopped herself down in her seat.

"Ladies and gentlemen," Peter began the act. "Behold—the Box of Death!" He made a grand gesture toward the box.

A snicker ran through the crowd.

"Laugh all you want," Peter shot back. "In just a few minutes, you'll be puking your guts up."

Mrs. Dingleman waved a disapproving finger at him. "Peter . . ."

"Sorry," Peter whispered to the principal. Then he turned his attention back to the crowd. "To prove to you what horrors await my assistant, I'll need a volunteer from the audience."

No one but Gerald MacDougal raised a hand.

"Gerald MacDougal," Peter announced. "Please step onto the stage."

Gerald clomped his way up to Peter, bagpipes and all.

"I'd like you to examine this sword," Peter said, pulling one from the bag.

Gerald felt the tip of the blade, then gently slid his finger down the side of it. "It's pretty sharp," he told the crowd.

"So sharp," Peter went on, "it will slice through this melon with one easy chop."

Bo handed a cantaloupe to Peter.

"You want me to chop it?" Gerald asked, breathing down Peter's neck.

Peter shook his head as he gave Gerald a shove. "Get off the stage now, Gerald," he said. "The volunteer part of the show is over."

Gerald clomped his way back to his seat as Peter lifted the sword over his head.

Chopping the melon in half had been Bo's idea. And it worked like a charm. As the audience watched Peter slice it in two, they were on the edge of their seats.

Peter smiled. "My assistant will now climb into the Box of Death and face this very same sword," he told the crowd.

Once Bo was positioned inside the box, Peter closed the lid. "Ready?" he whispered.

Bo nodded.

"Prepare to die, my friend!" Peter laughed maniacally as he swung the sword through the air.

"Wait!" Bo cried. "Don't do it!"

Peter could see the members of the audience holding their breath as he plunged the first sword through the box.

Bo let out a scream. The audience gave a collective gasp.

Peter slid another sword through. Then another. And another. With each one, the audience grew more and more horrified. Not only were they gasping, they were starting to cover their eyes.

"Now I will plunge the final sword through my assistant's heart!" Peter told the crowd.

As Peter slid the sword through the top of the box, Bo let the fountain of blood and his bloodcurdling scream rip, just as he had in the garage.

Mrs. Dingleman sprang from her seat, ready to race to the stage. "He's okay, Mrs. Dingleman," Peter assured her. "I swear. It's just an act," he whispered. "Remember?"

As Mrs. Dingleman sat back down, Peter grinned from ear to ear. Whether the judges liked it or not, they had to admit that Peter's act was more thrilling than anything they'd seen so far. And it wasn't over yet.

"I will now put my assistant out of his misery, by cutting him in half," Peter told the crowd.

He and Bo had added this part of the trick at the end of their practice session the previous night. All Bo had to do was stick a pair of fake feet out of the bottom of the box, then scrunch his body up to the top half, while Peter slid a big metal blade down the middle. Then he could separate the box in two pieces so that it looked like Bo really had been cut in half.

Peter picked up the blade and positioned it in the middle of the box.

"Give me a second," Bo whispered. "I'm not ready." Finally, Bo said, "Go."

Peter slid the blade through the center of the box, then unlatched the box and separated it into two pieces.

The audience went wild. So did the judges.

"We're definitely going home with those bikes now!" Bo exclaimed. "Just hurry up and get me out of this box. I've got a cramp in my leg."

"In a minute," Peter whispered. "I want to do one more trick," he said, putting the box back together again.

"What trick?" Bo asked.

"Just go with the flow," Peter told him. Then he produced another metal blade. "Now, for the grand finale," he shouted above the cheers of the crowd. "I will chop off my assistant's head!"

"Are you nuts?" Bo yelped. "We didn't practice this!"

"Just shut up," Peter told him. "I know what I'm doing."

Peter ignored Bo's protests and turned to the audience. He smiled out at the crowd of faces. He'd never been a star before. And it felt pretty good—until he slid the blade into the slot near Bo's throat.

Peter felt the blade hitting Bo's neck. Problem was, he didn't feel it retracting.

Bo started to scream bloody murder.

"Calm down," Peter whispered. "I'll pull it back out again!"

As Peter gripped the blade, he noticed that the stone in his ring was changing. The colors were swirling as violently as a tornado. Even without the magic wand, something was happening. Something bad.

Peter tugged furiously at the blade, but he couldn't make it budge. He tried to get a better grip, but the blade slipped away from him—all the way through Bo's neck.

Peter watched with horror as Bo's eyes rolled back in his head. Then his head fell back onto the table with a terrible thud.

21

I killed him!" Peter screamed at the audience. "His head and body are totally separated!"

The audience sprang to their feet, applauding wildly. "Great act, Peter!" they cheered. "You're better than Houdini!"

"This isn't an act!" Peter shouted. He was so terrified, the whole auditorium started to spin. "The blade chopped right through his throat! There's a huge space between his head and his shoulders!"

"Hey!" a voice from behind him shouted back. "Don't you think you're being a little melodramatic?"

Peter turned around. Bo was wide awake and

talking—at least his *head* was wide awake. The rest of him was still on its own.

"Bo, you're not going to believe this," Peter fumbled. "But you're not in one piece!"

"Neither is your brain," Bo replied.

"I'm serious," Peter said. But Bo was listening to the crowd cheer.

"Hurry up and get me out of here," Bo said. "So I can take a couple of bows."

"I can't!" Peter told him. "You're not all attached!"

"Cut it out already," Bo hissed. "We've milked this routine for all it's worth!"

Peter stood frozen.

"Fine," Bo huffed. "I'll do it myself."

Peter's heart stopped as Bo reached up to pull out the blade. He was terrified that once the blade was out, Bo's head would roll off the table and drop to the stage. But that didn't happen. Instead, Bo's head and shoulders seemed to magically reattach.

Peter stood dumbfounded as Bo pushed open the lid of the box and hopped out.

"Way to go, Bo!" the audience cheered.

"Bow, you idiot," Bo said, elbowing Peter in the ribs.

"Are you sure your head's okay?" Peter asked, bending at the waist.

"No," Bo answered. "It's swelling up."

"What do you mean?" Peter yelped.

"I mean, it's getting big from all this applause," Bo declared. "Isn't yours?"

Peter forced a smile and a nod.

As the next and final act was finally called to the stage, Peter and Bo took their seats. And while Bo watched the stage, Peter watched Bo, just to make sure he was still in one piece. But Bo seemed fine. In fact, he kept craning his neck around to shoot Mary-Margaret dirty looks.

Maybe I imagined it, Peter thought. *Maybe Bo's head didn't really come off. Maybe it was an optical illusion, just like Crazy Merlin's eyes.*

Either way, one thing was certain—Peter was never going to mess around with the Box of Death again. Besides, he wouldn't need to.

Ten minutes later, the bikes were in the bag.

"And the grand prize goes to . . ."

Peter and Bo ran for the stage before Mrs. Dingleman had even finished her sentence.

"Peter the Great," she continued. "And his Little Magic Act of Horrors."

As Bo tugged his ten-speed mountain bike out of Mrs. Dingleman's hands, he turned his attention to the second- and third-place losers, who were standing right next to him.

"Nice cuckoo clock you've got there, Mary-Margaret," Bo teased.

Mary-Margaret burst into tears.

The cuckoo clock was the prize for the second-place winner, Mary-Margaret and her baton-twirling hoedown routine. She also took third prize, a year's supply of pens from the school store, which she shared with Carol Ann.

After Mrs. Dingleman finished her little speech about how everyone who entered the competition was really a winner, Mary-Margaret stomped off the stage with her cuckoo clock. Peter and Bo strutted down the aisle behind her, showing off the grand prizes.

Peter and Bo couldn't wait to get the bikes outside so they could ride them. They had been so sure that they were going to win, they'd left their old bikes at home. Besides, Grandma Grussler had to drive them to school so that they could get the Box of Death to the auditorium. They were going to leave it there for the weekend, assuring Mrs. Dingleman that Grandma Grussler would pick it up Monday.

The moment Bo and Peter hit the outdoors, Bo hopped onto his bike and took off like a shot.

"Wait up!" Peter hurried to catch up.

"This bike rides like the wind. Watch this," Bo called over his shoulder. "I can even jump the curb."

Peter watched as Bo popped a wheelie up onto the sidewalk. Then he popped another, and landed back in the street. "Too cool, huh?" he said, turning to look at Peter.

It was cool. And Peter was just about to try it himself, when Bo hit a pothole so hard, the back end of his bike flew a foot in the air.

But the bike wasn't the only thing that went flying.

Bo's head flew right off his shoulders.

22

Peter watched in horror as Bo's head flew through the air and sailed over his own head.

"Aaaaaaaggghhh!" Peter screamed as he ducked.

"Aaaaaaaggghhh!" Bo's head echoed back. A second later, it landed with a sickening *plop* on the strip of grass between the curb and the sidewalk.

Peter couldn't believe that Bo's head was screaming. But even more unbelievable was the fact that Bo's body just kept pedaling away on his bicycle as if nothing had happened.

Peter didn't know what to do first. Should he go back and get Bo's head, or keep going to catch his body?

He didn't have to think about it very long. The answer was simple. Bo's head wasn't going anywhere. Peter had to go after the rest of him.

Bo's body had a pretty good lead, but it wasn't going very fast. Peter caught up before the end of the block.

"Bo," Peter called out as he came up beside him.

"I'm back here!" Bo's head shouted. "Help me!"

"I'm trying!" Peter yelled over his shoulder.

Bo's body kept right on going.

Peter jumped off his own bike and ran after Bo. When he caught up, he reached out and grabbed Bo's handlebars and held on tight. He managed to stop the bike and keep it upright so that Bo's body didn't topple to the ground, but his legs kept pedaling. After a few seconds, they stopped, and his body sat quietly.

Peter helped Bo off the bike. It was then that he saw the stump where Bo's neck should have been.

It wasn't mangled and bloody, the way Peter thought it would be. Instead, it looked like the stump that's left when a mannequin's head comes off. But this wasn't a mannequin's body. It was Bo's body! And the sight of it headless made Peter sick.

Bo's head sat half a block back in the grass, still screaming.

"What's going on?" Bo's head cried frantically. "Help me!"

"I'm coming," Peter shouted. He grabbed Bo's arm and began pulling his body toward his head. Luckily, the body followed obediently.

As Peter and Bo's body approached Bo's head, Bo began yelling even more hysterically.

"What's happened to me?" Bo shrieked. But he didn't give Peter a chance to answer. The questions just kept pouring out. "How did my head fall off? How come I'm not dead?"

"Calm down!" Peter commanded. He was feeling anything but calm himself. He just wanted Bo to be quiet. The last thing he wanted to do was attract any attention.

"Calm down?" Bo yelled. "How am I supposed to calm down? Look at me! How did this happen to me?"

"I tried to tell you before," Peter said, more loudly than he'd meant to. He looked around quickly to make sure that no one was listening. They were still alone.

"I think the magic worked again," he said. "When I

took your head off, I really took your head off. But then I thought maybe I only imagined it because you seemed to be okay after the trick was over."

"Well, I'm not okay, am I?" Bo hollered. "I told you I didn't want to do this magic show. Now look what's happened."

"We'll find a way to fix it," Peter said as he bent down to pick up Bo's head.

"Stay away from me," Bo shouted. "What are you going to do to me now?"

Peter picked up Bo's head and placed it back on his shoulders. "I'm putting you back together," he said. "There, how does that feel?"

"It feels like you're holding me together!" Bo snapped.

Peter took his hands away from Bo's neck—slowly. Then he took a step back.

Bo's head stayed in place.

"You see!" Peter exclaimed. "You're back in one piece."

But Bo wanted to see for himself. He bent his head forward to look down at his body—and his head rolled right off his shoulders again.

"I'm going to kill you for this!" Bo's head went nuts as his body stamped its feet.

"Stop screaming!" Peter pleaded with Bo as he bent down to pick up his head from the grass. "It's not helping one bit."

Bo kept screaming anyway.

"We're just going to have to hold it on until we figure out what to do," Peter said, plopping Bo's head back onto his shoulders. He was nowhere near as gentle as he had been the last time.

"Ouch," Bo complained, reaching up to take charge of his own head.

"We've got to get back to my house," Peter told Bo. "You hold your head. I'll bring the bikes."

They were only a few blocks away from home. They walked the short distance in silence, giving Peter a chance to think. By the time they'd reached his garage, he had the whole thing figured out.

"It's going to be okay," Peter assured Bo.

"Sure it is," Bo grumbled. "For you, maybe."

"Listen to me, " Peter said. "This magic stuff doesn't

work for good. It only lasts a little while, like it did with Tiger and Mary-Margaret."

"So what am I supposed to do?" Bo asked. "Sit around and wait for the magic spell to wear off?"

"What else can we do?" Peter said.

"I can't keep holding my head on like this. My arms are getting tired," Bo complained.

"Maybe we could glue it on with airplane glue," Peter suggested.

"No way!" Bo protested. "You're not supposed to use that stuff on your skin. It's poison."

Peter looked around the garage for another solution. There had to be something that would keep Bo's head on his shoulders for a little while. "Duct tape!" Peter exclaimed. He'd spotted a roll of it on his father's workbench, and he headed over to get it. "My dad uses this stuff for everything," he told Bo.

Bo stepped back as Peter approached him with the tape. "I don't know about this," he said.

"Come on," Peter coaxed, unwinding the tape. "I'm telling you, it'll work great."

It took a whole roll of tape, but eventually Bo's head was firmly fastened to his neck. Unfortunately, Bo couldn't move it at all.

"This is terrible," Bo moaned.

"It'll do for now," Peter said. "We just can't let anybody see you like this."

"So what am I supposed to do, hide in the garage?" Bo asked.

"No," Peter answered. "We'll sneak up to my room and stay there until your head gets reattached."

Peter was convinced that Bo would be back to normal in no time, just like Tiger and Mary-Margaret. But by dinnertime, normal still hadn't happened.

Bo refused to go home with his head taped on. His parents would freak out, he said.

Luckily it was Friday so he and Peter arranged for him to have dinner and spend the night at Peter's house.

The problem was that Grandma Grussler insisted that they eat dinner at the kitchen table with her. Peter didn't know how they were going to hide Bo's condition from her. They hadn't found a solution yet when Grandma

Grussler burst into Peter's bedroom to announce that dinner was on the table.

"Good gracious," she gasped, staring at Bo. "What on earth do you have around your neck, young man?"

"Uh . . ." Peter tried to think up some kind of answer. Bo just stood there dumbfounded.

"Don't tell me," Grandma Grussler went on. "It's some new fashion statement, right? Like having your nose pierced. Or shaving your head." She looked at Bo more closely and shook her head. "I can't imagine that this is going to catch on," she said. "But what do I know? Now come and eat."

Peter and Bo followed her downstairs, exchanging looks of amazement and amusement. Nothing seemed to faze Grandma Grussler. She lived in her own little world. It was a good thing, too.

During dinner, Peter and Bo pretended to be interested as Grandma Grussler went on and on about all the things that were in style when she was a kid. Grandma Grussler was so lost in her stories that she didn't notice what was happening to Bo.

Bo didn't notice, either. He was happily wolfing down his spaghetti and meatballs. But Peter dropped his fork in horror.

A stain was spreading across the front of Bo's shirt. It was getting bigger by the minute. It was bright red—the color of blood.

23

Peter put his hand to his mouth to hold back a scream.

What was going on? What was happening to Bo now?

The bright red liquid was oozing out from under the duct tape around Bo's neck. But it wasn't blood. It was spaghetti and sauce. Bo was swallowing, but his food wasn't making it to his stomach.

Peter had to stop Bo from eating. And he had to find a way to do it without making Grandma Grussler suspicious.

He coughed.

Nobody paid attention.

He did it again.

Still nothing. Bo went right on eating. And Grandma Grussler went right on talking. Neither one stopped until their plates were clean.

"Would anyone like some dessert?" Grandma Grussler asked as she got up to begin clearing the table.

Bo was about to say yes, but Peter interrupted him. "Maybe later, Grandma," he said. "May we be excused now, please?"

He didn't wait for her answer. He grabbed Bo, pulled him from his chair, and dragged him out of the kitchen, leaving a trail of spaghetti behind them.

"Hey!" Bo protested. "I wanted dessert. I'm still starving."

"No kidding," Peter said. "None of the food made it to your stomach."

Bo looked down at the front of his shirt, and his eyes almost popped out of his head. "This is terrible," he groaned. "I'm not ever going to get better, am I? What's going to happen to me?"

"You're going to be fine," Peter insisted. He dragged Bo upstairs to his bedroom. "It's just going to take a little more time. I think we ought to just watch some TV and go to bed. When we wake up in the morning, you'll be good as new."

"What if I'm not?" Bo worried.

"You will be," Peter said. "You have to be."

24

It didn't work!" Bo cried. "I'm still like the headless horseman! And I don't even have a horse!"

Peter winced the moment he opened his eyes. Bo's head was lying on the pillow next to his, screaming in his face. But the rest of Bo was lying on the floor.

"You said I'd be better by morning!" Bo continued to rant.

"Calm down," Peter told him, although he was close to panic himself. "Maybe it's just going to take a little bit longer."

"Like how long?" Bo shot back. "The rest of my life?"

Peter gulped at the thought.

"And what am I supposed to be when I grow up, huh? A circus freak? A human bowling ball?" Bo's brain was spinning out of control.

So was Peter's—until he landed on a solution. "Crazy Merlin!" He blurted it out to Bo.

"What?" Bo barked. "You want me to be Crazy Merlin when I grow up?"

"No." Peter shook his head. "All we have to do is go back to Crazy Merlin. I bet you a million dollars he can fix this."

Bo's eyes lit up, and his body sprang to its feet. "I bet he can!" Bo agreed. "Tape me back up and let's go!"

When Peter finished taping Bo's throat to the stump of his neck, he and Bo headed downstairs to tell Grandma Grussler not to bother with breakfast. Peter said that they wanted to go outside for some exercise first. Grandma Grussler thought it was a "healthy" idea.

"Wait a minute," Bo said as they started out the front door. "I can't go outside looking like this. Grandma Grussler may think that a duct-taped neck is a fashion statement, but no one else will."

"Wait here," Peter said. "I'll get you a turtleneck."

"A turtleneck," Bo moaned. "It's three thousand degrees out."

"You're just going to have to deal with it until we get to Crazy Merlin's," Peter told him. Then he ran back up to his room and dug one out of his closet. He also dug out the phone book to make sure he had the address right.

"That's weird," Peter said, scanning the yellow pages. The full-page ad for the Little Magic Shop of Horrors was nowhere to be seen. And there wasn't a single page torn out of the book, either. It was as if the ad had never existed.

Maybe this is a different phone book, Peter told himself. He knew it wasn't true, but there was no time to worry about the missing ad now. Bo's shoulders were missing something a lot bigger.

"I know it was 101 Nosuch Place," Peter said, thinking aloud as he ran back downstairs. "That's definitely the address."

The second the turtleneck was over Bo's neck, they were out the door and running. Peter didn't want to take the bikes; he was afraid that Bo's head would go flying again, right in the middle of town.

Unfortunately, Bo's head fell off anyway—six times. Between the heat from the sun and the turtleneck, Bo was sweating like crazy. The glue on the tape was melting away. So Bo had to walk down Main Street holding his head on.

Unfortunately, that was the least of their problems.

"It's not here," Bo cried, staring at the solid brick wall between the bookstore and the ladies' shoe shop. "The archway's not here."

"Maybe we're in the wrong spot," Peter suggested, even though he knew they weren't.

"We're not in the wrong spot!" Bo snapped. "The alleyway was right between these two stores!"

"Don't panic." Peter tried to sound calm. "Maybe Crazy Merlin moved down the street."

"With an entire alleyway?" Bo shot back.

Peter headed into the bookstore. "Maybe somebody here can tell us where Crazy Merlin is."

"Excuse me," Peter said as he walked up to the clerk at the front counter. "Can you tell me where the Little Magic Shop of Horrors is?"

"Sorry," the clerk answered. "I've never heard of it."

"It used to be right around the corner at 101 Nosuch Place," Peter told him. "Down an alleyway."

"What alleyway?" the clerk asked.

"The one that was right next door to your store!" Bo practically shouted.

"I hate to tell you this, kid," the clerk responded sharply. "But there has never been an alleyway next to this store. And I know for sure that there's no such place as Nosuch Place. Not in this town, anyway."

Peter's heart sank to the pit of his stomach.

The ad in the phone book wasn't the only thing that was missing. So was the Little Magic Shop of Horrors.

25

Things couldn't get any worse, or so Peter and Bo thought. But when they got back to Peter's house, Grandma Grussler was waiting for them on the front porch, and she had some very bad news.

"You boys had a visitor while you were gone," she told them.

"A visitor?" Peter asked. "Who was it?"

"Give me a minute." Grandma Grussler scratched her head. "I can't seem to remember his name. But he said he worked at your school."

"Janitor Bob!" Peter and Bo gasped in unison. It was Saturday, the day they were supposed to serve detention with Janitor Bob. With everything that had happened, they'd completely forgotten about him.

"He's not going to come back here, is he?" Bo asked.

"He didn't say so," Grandma Grussler answered. "But he might. He said he would catch up with the two of you later."

"Great." Peter groaned. "This is just great."

"Where did Janitor Bob go after he left here?" Bo asked.

"Beats me," Grandma Grussler told him. Then she got up to head back inside the house. "I guess he went home."

"Good," Peter said after Grandma Grussler closed the door behind her. "Because you and I have to go to school."

"Are you crazy?" Bo said. "Why do you want to go to school? So we can do our detention all alone?"

"No," Peter answered. "So we can put you back into the magic box. That's where your head came off in the first place," he said. "So maybe if we stick you back in there, we can put it back on. It's our only hope."

"It won't work," Bo said hopelessly. "I'm going to have to spend the rest of my life like this." His head began to sag. He pushed it back up again. The tape wasn't helping at all anymore.

"We've got to try," Peter told him.

Bo's head nodded, but not in agreement. He reached up with both hands to hold it onto his shoulders. "Fine." He sighed after a minute. "At this point, I'll try anything."

When the two of them got to the school, they found all the doors locked.

"Now what?" Bo asked. He'd given up trying to hold his head on his shoulders. He was carrying it under his arm.

"Let's look for an open window," Peter suggested.

"And if we don't find one?" Bo was being totally negative.

"Then we'll break one." Peter's nerves were just frayed enough to do it, too.

Luckily, he didn't have to break a window. There was a whole wall of open windows at the back of the school.

"Come on," Peter called to Bo, who was having a tough time keeping up. "We can climb in through one of these windows."

Peter stood watching impatiently as Bo plodded toward him, still carrying his head under his arm.

"I'll go in first, then I'll help you," Peter told him.

The windows were high enough off the ground that Peter had to use both arms to lift himself up and over the ledge. Once inside, he turned back to Bo. "Give me your head," he said. "I'll hold it while you climb in."

Bo handed it over, and Peter stepped away from the window to give Bo's body room to get inside.

But as Bo was climbing through the window, something caught Peter's eye. Something was moving down the hallway toward him. He spun to face it, terrified that it was Janitor Bob, waiting to ambush them.

But it wasn't a person at all.

What Peter saw startled him so badly that he dropped Bo's head and stood frozen as it rolled away.

26

Bo's head started screaming as it rolled down the hall. "Help me! Help me!"

But Peter just stood there staring at what was going on around him. It couldn't be real. He had to be imagining things.

Peter blinked hard, trying to erase the image from his brain. But when he opened his eyes again, it was still there.

A few feet in front of Peter, a broom was sweeping the hallway—all by itself!

At the end of the hall, a giant floor-waxing machine hummed away, polishing the floor to a glossy finish. No one was operating it. The machine ran on its own. It wasn't even plugged into an electrical outlet.

A feather duster swished back and forth, cleaning the tops of the lockers, while a squeegee worked on the windows.

"What's going on?" Peter gasped. He took a step back. He was about to turn and run.

But someone blocked his path.

Peter let out a scream as he bumped into Bo's headless body.

He couldn't run away—not without Bo.

"Peter!" Bo's head shouted. "Come get me!"

But just as Peter moved to retrieve Bo's head, the floor-waxing machine smashed into it and sent it rolling around the corner. Bo's head disappeared down a dark corridor.

Peter had no choice but to follow. He stepped around the sweeping broom and made his way down the hall.

"Bo!" Peter called.

There was no answer.

The floor-waxing machine moved toward him, blocking his path.

Peter took a step to his right. The machine moved in front of him. He moved to his left. The machine followed. He faked a right, then dove to the left, slipping past the machine by inches.

Now the machine was after him.

Peter tried to run, but the floor was too slippery.

"Bo!" Peter cried.

Still there was no answer.

Peter made it to the end of the hallway with the floor-waxing machine on his tail.

He grabbed the corner of the wall to propel himself around it. But as he made the turn, he was stopped dead in his tracks.

There was no way to make it past what blocked his way now. And no way to escape!

27

"Are you looking for this?"

Peter went pale as Janitor Bob held up Bo's head by a fistful of hair.

"Answer me, boy," Janitor Bob ordered.

Peter was so terrified, he could barely manage a nod.

"I ought to do this to you, you know," Janitor Bob threatened. "I ought to chop off your head, just like your buddy's here. Then I'd be done with you both."

Peter gulped so hard, he nearly swallowed his tongue. Janitor Bob really was a psycho! He was standing there, swinging Bo's head around like it was no big deal, and he was threatening to chop off Peter's, too!

"And let me tell you something, mister," Janitor Bob warned Bo. "If you don't quiet your screaming head down, I'll chop out that tongue of yours, too."

Bo's head shut up. But his body kept running—right for the door.

"You'd better stop him," Janitor Bob told Peter. "Otherwise, there's going to be two of you running around these halls like chickens without heads."

As Peter turned to go after Bo's body, he considered running straight out the door. At least then he'd be a chicken who still had a head. But there was no way he could leave Bo behind. He grabbed Bo's arm and stopped his body.

"Now we're going to take a little walk," Janitor Bob told them. "Down to my office."

"For what?" Bo yelped as Janitor Bob carried his head down the hallway. "What are you going to do?"

"A magic act," Janitor Bob answered. "And I'm not even going to need the Box of Death to do it." He looked at Peter menacingly.

What the heck is that supposed to mean? Peter's brain started spinning faster than the floor-waxer. *How does he* know about the Box of Death? He wasn't even at the talent show. And what kind of "magic act" is he talking about? Making us disappear forever?

"'Peter the Great,'" Janitor Bob continued to rant as he unlocked the door to the basement. "The great what? Moron?"

Peter gulped again.

"Let me tell you something, boy," Janitor Bob went on. "Next time you go shopping for something, it ought to be a brain. Now get down those stairs." He shoved Peter and Bo's body through the doorway. Then he followed them down to the basement, carrying Bo's head under his arm like a football.

As soon as Janitor Bob opened his office door, Peter saw the Box of Death. Piled on top of it were the swords and the chopping blades, shined up and sharpened.

Bo saw them, too. "I thought you said you weren't going to use that," his head blurted out in a panic.

"I'm not," Janitor Bob replied, setting Bo's head down on his desk. "And neither are the two of you—ever again."

Ever again! Peter gave Bo's head a worried look. No doubt about it, Janitor Bob was planning to kill them.

"Now, before I do some hoodoo of my own," Janitor Bob said, locking the door behind Peter, "why don't you two tell me just where you disappeared to this morning."

Peter was about to make up a story, but what was the point? In a few minutes he'd be dead, so why not just spill his guts before Janitor Bob ripped them out?

"We were trying to fix up Bo's head," Peter started to explain. "So we decided to go back to the Little Magic Shop of Horrors. That's where we bought all this stuff."

"No such place," Janitor Bob said, shaking his head.

"There is too!" Bo told him. "At least there was."

Janitor Bob smirked.

"We're telling the truth," Peter insisted. "There was such a place."

"I know," he replied. "I've been there myself. You can buy yourself a lifetime of horrors at 101 Nosuch Place."

"Wait a minute," Bo jumped in. "You know where it is?"

"Not anymore," Janitor Bob answered. "And if you think for a second that *you're* going to find it again, you're missing more than your butt. You're missing your mind."

Peter was getting more and more confused by the second. "Then you know Crazy Merlin?" he asked.

"Sure," Janitor Bob answered. "But I haven't seen hide nor hair of that creep in thirty years. If I did, I'd pop out more than his eyeballs."

"Can you help us find him?" Peter asked.

"He's not even flesh and blood anymore," Janitor Bob said. "He's just an illusion. Even after death, that madman is still working magic."

"Crazy Merlin's dead?" Bo gasped. "We bought a magic kit from a dead magician?"

Janitor Bob nodded. "I wish he'd appear to me again," he growled. "I'd wave my wand in his face and show him some real horrors."

"You have a wand?" Peter asked nervously.

"Got yours, too," he said, picking it up from the desk.

No way! Peter panicked. *Bob's not just a psycho janitor. He's a psycho janitor magician!*

"You're a magician like Crazy Merlin?" Bo asked him.

"Better," Janitor Bob declared. "Because *I'm* not insane. And I'm still flesh and blood."

Could have fooled me, Peter thought—at least the part about being sane.

Bo must have been thinking the same thing. His head blurted a blunder. "Then how come you're planning to kill us?"

Janitor Bob started to laugh—insanely. "Is that what you think I'm going to do? Kill you?"

Peter nodded for both of them.

Janitor Bob kept laughing. "I'm going to kill you, all right," he said. "With kindness. Even after all the grief you've put me through."

Peter watched as Janitor Bob pulled off his work gloves and threw them down on the desk. There, on Janitor Bob's right hand, was a ring identical to the one Crazy Merlin had given Peter. The ring that was still stuck on his finger.

Bo saw it, too. "Look," he said to Peter. "Janitor Bob has your ring."

"It's *my* ring," Janitor Bob corrected. "But I want the one *you're* wearing, too," he told Peter.

"For what?" Peter asked.

"For insurance," Janitor Bob told him. "Because your buddy's not leaving here in one piece until I have it."

"What are you saying?" Bo exclaimed. "That you're going to put me back together?"

"Not until I have that ring, I'm not," Janitor Bob answered.

"You can do that?" Peter asked. "You can fix him?"

"In the blink of an eye," Janitor Bob answered. "Took me thirty years to figure my way around the horrors I bought from Crazy Merlin. But I did it. And unless you want to spend the next thirty years figuring it out for yourself," he said, "you'll give me that ring."

"I can't," Peter told him, tugging at his finger. "It's stuck. I can't get it off."

"I can." Janitor Bob grinned. Then he headed over to the Box of Death and picked up one of the chopping blades.

"What are you going to do?" Peter swallowed hard.

"Cut it off," Janitor Bob answered.

"The ring?" Peter asked.

"No," Janitor Bob replied. "Your finger."

28

Peter crammed his fingers into his pocket. "No way you're chopping me into tiny little pieces!" he cried. "That's not killing me with kindness! That's killing me with a lot of pain."

"Give him your hand," Bo's head fumed from the top of the desk. "What's the big deal?"

"Are you nuts?" Peter snapped. "He wants to chop off my finger!"

"Hello!" Bo shot back. "You're talking to a head here, remember? Seems to me that if Janitor Bob is willing to exchange your finger for my head, you ought to do it."

Peter knew he had no choice but to hold out his trembling hand.

Janitor Bob grabbed it by the wrist and slapped it down on top of the desk, next to Bo's head.

"Aw, man." Bo's face cringed. "I can't watch this."

"Fine," Janitor Bob said. He lifted Bo's head and slid it under the desk. "Ready?" he asked Peter.

No, I'm not ready! Peter wanted to scream. *How can anybody be ready to get his finger chopped off?* But he nodded instead.

"Trust me," Janitor Bob assured him. "You're not going to feel a thing."

Peter quickly turned his head as Janitor Bob picked up the blade and positioned it right above Peter's knuckle. At any moment he would feel the metal cutting through his flesh, hear it sawing through his bone.

Peter almost passed out. But he didn't feel another thing. The next sound he heard was Janitor Bob.

"Dang," Janitor Bob huffed. "This is one fat finger."

"What's the matter?" Peter yelped. "The blade won't go through?"

"No," Janitor Bob told him. "Your finger's already off. It's the ring I'm having a problem with."

Peter opened one eye and peeked down at his hand. Sure enough, his index finger was off. And the splice at his knuckle looked just like Bo's neck, even and smooth.

"Got it." Janitor Bob finally tugged the ring off and put it in his pocket. "Pretty cool, huh?" he said, waving Peter's finger in front of his nose.

Peter nodded, trying not to throw up.

"Told you it was easy," Janitor Bob said.

"Now you're going to put it back on, right?" Peter asked.

"After I get one last thing," Janitor Bob replied.

Peter's heart sank into his churning stomach. "We had a deal," he cried. "You said that once you got the ring off, you'd fix things."

"I said I'd fix your buddy's head," Janitor Bob corrected him. "And I will."

"But you're not going to fix my finger?" Peter said.

"Not until you give me the last tool of the trade," Janitor Bob told him.

"And what's that?" Peter asked.

"The amulet," he replied. "The one you got from Crazy Merlin."

"I don't have it," Peter said. "It's at home."

"It should have been around your neck," Janitor Bob growled. "That way, you could have saved yourself and me all kinds of aggravation."

"What kind of aggravation?" Peter wanted to know.

"All of it," Janitor Bob answered. "You never, ever mess around with magic unless you've got total control. And there's no way to have total control if you're not wearing this." Janitor Bob pulled a chain from under his shirt. Dangling on the end of it was an amulet.

"You've already got an amulet," Peter said. "Why do you need mine?"

"I don't *need* it," Janitor Bob explained. "I want it. It doesn't belong in the hands of an amateur. And only an amateur tries to do magic without using the most important tool of the trade. The amulet is more powerful than the wand and the ring combined. Without it, there's no way to protect or direct the forces that be."

"So what are you saying?" Peter asked. "If I'd worn

the amulet, the magic would have worked the way I wanted it to?"

"Yup," Janitor Bob answered. "With a little bit of practice, it's pretty much that simple."

"So why didn't Crazy Merlin tell me that?" Peter asked.

"He did," Janitor Bob replied. "But you thought the amulet was too goofy to wear, didn't you?"

Peter nodded.

"Don't feel so bad," Janitor Bob said. "That's exactly what Crazy Merlin wanted to have happen. He loves to wreak havoc. And he knows that nobody wants to wear a goofy necklace. Same thing happened to me when I was twelve. I didn't wear the necklace, either. I made one big mess with that wand and that ring. I even turned my cat into a tiger."

"Me too!" Peter exclaimed. "But he turned back again."

"You're lucky," Janitor Bob said. "When you don't know how to control the magic, sometimes it wears off, and sometimes it doesn't. Peanut, my cat, ended up at the zoo, hunting down zebras."

"I told you!" Bo's head screamed from under the desk. "I told you tigers eat zebras."

Janitor Bob chuckled as he lifted Bo's head from the floor. "I almost forgot about you," he said.

"Tell me about it," Bo grumbled.

"So are you ready to be put back together again?"

"More than ready," Bo said. "If I don't get to eat something soon, *I'm* going to end up at the zoo hunting zebras."

"Here." Janitor Bob handed Peter his finger. "Hold this for a second."

For some reason, carrying around Bo's head was nowhere near as creepy as holding his own finger. Peter couldn't help but cringe.

"I'm going to need the wand for this," Janitor Bob said, placing Bo's head on his shoulders. He picked one up from his desk and pointed it at Bo's throat.

Within seconds, the amulet on Janitor Bob's chest was glowing like a neon sign. He mumbled some mumbo jumbo and in the blink of an eye, Bo was back together again.

"You did it!" Bo exclaimed, springing up from the chair. "Look," he said. "I can even bend over."

"You can do a headstand, too, if you want," Janitor Bob told him. "When I fix things, I fix them right."

"What about my finger?" Peter asked sheepishly.

"Bring me the amulet, and I'll fix that up, too."

"Wait a minute." Peter suddenly had an idea. "If you give me back my ring and my wand, I can fix it myself, huh?"

"Over your dead body," Janitor Bob shot back. "You even think the word 'magic' again, and I swear I'll do worse than kill you. You got me?"

Peter nodded nervously. "I just thought I could save you the trouble, that's all."

Janitor Bob looked at him. "I'll tell you what," he said. "I'm going to put your finger back on. But if you're not back here with that amulet in less than an hour, I'll take ten of them off—without even leaving my office. Understood?"

"Deal," Peter said, handing Janitor Bob his finger. It was back on in a wink.

"Now move it," Janitor Bob ordered.

Peter headed for the door with Bo by his side. "Thanks, Janitor Bob." He smiled.

"I want to see how much you're going to be thanking me next Saturday," he said, "when you're washing all the windows in this building."

"Aw, man," Bo groaned under his breath. "Can't he just wash them magically, like he did with the floor?"

"Don't do it," Janitor Bob warned. "Don't try my patience worse than you already have. Now get going! Before I break my own rules and spill some blood. Namely yours."

Bo took off like a rocket with Peter burning rubber behind him.

29

Where could that stupid thing be?" Peter wondered. He and Bo had torn apart the garage looking for the magic amulet. But it was nowhere to be found.

"Maybe it's disappeared all by itself," Bo suggested.

"That's impossible," Peter told him. "It's got to be here somewhere. And we've got to find it. I want that thing out of my house."

"Maybe Grandma Grussler knows where it is," Bo said.

Peter doubted it. But at least they could get her to help them look for it. "Let's go ask her," he said to Bo.

Peter threw open the door that led from the garage

to the house. "Grandma!" he called as he stepped inside.

Bo was right behind him. "Grandma Grussler!" he echoed Peter.

There was no answer.

"Grandma!" Peter called again as they headed toward the family room.

The TV was blaring.

"No wonder she's not answering," Bo said. "She's got the TV so loud she can't possibly hear us."

But Grandma Grussler wasn't in the family room watching TV.

Tiger was. He sat on the couch all by himself, staring at the screen.

"Hey Tiger, where's Grandma?" Peter said, not really expecting an answer.

He got one anyway. Tiger looked him right in the eye and let out the most pitiful cry Peter had ever heard. Then Tiger looked back at the TV and cried again.

"What's wrong with the cat?" Bo asked.

Peter just shrugged. He didn't have time to worry about Tiger. He had to find the amulet. He was about to call out for his grandmother again when he realized that she would never hear him over the noise of the TV.

The remote control was on the couch beside Tiger. Peter grabbed it and aimed it at the set. He was just about to hit the mute button when something stopped him.

Peter gasped.

"What is it?" Bo asked.

Peter was too stunned to answer. He just stood there, staring at the TV.

"So, Grandma Grussler," the host of *Global Gladiators* said, "how did you come to be on our show today?"

The camera was on Grandma Grussler. She was on TV—on her favorite game show, standing right next to the pip-squeak from Poughkeepsie. But she looked pretty confused.

"Well, I'm not exactly sure how I got here," she answered. "I was just sitting on the couch watching the show with my little Tiger, and I said, 'I wish *I* were on *Global Gladiators*.' And the next thing you know, here I am."

The game show host laughed as if Grandma Grussler were kidding him.

But Peter knew that Grandma Grussler wasn't kidding. She really didn't know how she'd gotten there.

But Peter did.

Grandma Grussler was wearing the magic amulet.

Don't miss the next spine-tingling book
in the DEADTIME STORIES® series

GRANDPA'S MONSTER MOVIES

Catan Thomas was lost—hopelessly lost.

Worse than that, he was being hunted.

He thought he was well hidden. But then, so were his hunters.

They might be anywhere, Catan Thomas thought. *They might be just a few feet away right now!*

There was no way for him to know. He couldn't see more than a foot in any direction, because he was deep inside a cornfield, surrounded by stalks that towered high above his head.

It had seemed like the perfect place to hide. But now he wasn't so sure. Now he felt swallowed up by the field.

The cornstalks stood so close together that Catan Thomas could barely move between them. Still he kept going, hoping that eventually he would make it to safety.

He tried to be quiet. But he couldn't avoid rustling the leaves of the plants as he passed by them.

He was aware of every sound he made. In a way, that made him feel safe. He figured that if *he* couldn't move through the cornfield without making noise, neither could anyone else. No one would be able to catch him off guard.

Unless they were sitting quietly, waiting!

That thought stopped Catan Thomas dead in his tracks.

Now what? he thought.

Before he could decide, he heard a sudden rustle and was grabbed from behind.

"Aaaggghhh!" he screamed.

A hand closed over his mouth.

"Shut up," a voice commanded.

He did as he was told.

"It's just me, C.T.," the voice whispered in his ear.

It took him a moment to realize that the voice belonged to his cousin, Lea Rose.

"They almost got me," she told him as she removed her hand from his mouth.

"How did you get away?" he asked.

"I ran!" she said as if he were stupid. "I don't know if they followed me, but I don't think we should stay here. We've got to keep moving!"

"Yeah," C.T. agreed. "But which way?"

Lea Rose shrugged hopelessly.

"This is a nightmare," C.T. said. "We're being stalked in a cornfield."

"By a bunch of hillbillies," Lea Rose added.

"The worst part is that we're actually related to those hillbillies." C.T. groaned.

"They're *distant* cousins," Lea Rose reminded him.

"Not distant enough," C.T. complained. "I wish I'd never met these people. I'm never coming to another family reunion as long as I live."

"I know what you mean," Lea Rose agreed. "I can't believe we have to spend another two whole days here in Bumbleweed. I don't know how Grandma and Grandpa can stand to live out here in the middle of nowhere. They don't even have cable. Who lives without cable?" Lea Rose shook her head in disbelief.

"For real," C.T. agreed. "And forget about trying to use your cell phone out here. It's impossible. I can't believe your mom and my dad grew up on this farm, too."

Lea's mom and C.T.'s dad were Grandma and Grandpa's children. They were the *normal* side of the family. The problem was that Grandpa had two brothers— Ernie and Earl—who weren't very normal at all.

Ernie was the youngest brother. He'd been struck by lightning—sixteen different times. It was amazing that Ernie had even survived. But aside from lightning bolt number two, which left Uncle Ernie with a "hair condition," and lightning bolt number nine, which gave him a "kick," Uncle Ernie claimed to be fine. Still, the rest of the family was quite clear on the fact that Uncle Ernie had sixteen holes in his head.

But Uncle Ernie wasn't nearly as big a problem as Earl,

Grandpa's middle brother, because Uncle Ernie wasn't married. He lived with Grandma and Grandpa in their gigantic old farmhouse. And *he* didn't have any kids.

Uncle Earl, the "raving maniac," *was* married. He and his wife, Luleen, had lots of kids, and lots of grandchildren—C.T. and Lea's *distant* cousins. Cousins that C.T. and Lea were forced to be nice to.

That was the real problem. Because the cousins were a *real* scary bunch.

"We don't have time to stand around talking," Lea said. "We've got to find our way back to the house before those freaks catch up to us."

She shoved C.T. to get him moving.

But C.T. stood frozen right where he was.

"Listen," he whispered to Lea.

They heard the rustle of cornstalks.

Someone was headed toward them, but C.T. couldn't figure out from which direction. They had to know that before they started running. C.T. wanted to make sure they were running *away* from the drooling stalkers and not toward them.

Lea pointed to the right.

C.T. listened for another moment and decided she was right. He grabbed her hand and started running to the left.

But as they ran, whoever was chasing them began moving more quickly.

C.T. heard the stalks cracking and pulled Lea along even faster. But he knew they weren't going to get away this time.

Their pursuer was gaining on them with lightning speed.

C.T. looked back over his shoulder.

Less than ten feet behind them, he saw the cornstalks part as they broke and fell.

But nobody was there.

It was as if an invisible force was causing the damage.

"What's going on?" C.T. cried as he kept running.

The cornstalks behind them continued to snap and fall. Whatever was chasing them was about to overtake them.

It was only about six feet away when C.T. finally saw what was after them. It was like nothing he'd ever seen in his life. And it definitely wasn't one of his cousins!

ABOUT THE AUTHORS

As sisters, Annette and Gina Cascone share the same last name. As writers, they sometimes share the same brain. As children, they found it difficult to share anything at all.

The Cascone sisters grew up in Lawrenceville, New Jersey. It was there that Annette and Gina began making up stories. Since their father was a criminal attorney, and their mother claimed to have ESP, the Cascone sisters honed their storytelling skills early on in life—mainly to stay out of trouble. These days, they're telling their crazy stories to anyone who will listen.

Here are the stats: Gina is older; Annette is not. Gina

is married; Annette should be. Gina has two children; Annette borrowed one. Gina has a granddaughter; Annette has a grandniece. Gina has cats; Annette has dogs. They both have a sister named Elise.

Visit Annette and Gina at www.agcascone.com.